FREELAN...

FREELANCE DEATH

Andrew Taylor

GOLLANCZ CRIME

For Blaise

First published in Great Britain 1987
by Victor Gollancz Ltd

First VG Crime edition published 1993
by Victor Gollancz
A Cassell imprint
Villiers House, 41/47 Strand, London WC2N 5JE

© Andrew Taylor 1987

A catalogue record for this book
is available from the British Library

ISBN 0 575 05567 7

Printed and bound in Great Britain
by Cox & Wyman Ltd, Reading

Prologue

TROUBLES NEVER CAME singly. When Mrs Harvey broke her teacup in the washing-up bowl, she knew that something else would go wrong before the day was out.

On Thursdays she had tea with Miss Pope at the Alexandra Hotel. It was 150 yards from her flat to the hotel. At this time of year the wind whipped along the sea-front in a positive gale. It was treacherous underfoot. The Council never dealt adequately with snow and ice. Mrs Harvey derived a grim pleasure from the thought that when the Councillors were Senior Citizens (*risible* term) themselves, they would suffer in their turn.

As she picked her way along the deserted Promenade, the salt stung her lips. The tide was high; it sucked greedily at the shingle. The sea, devoid of shipping, stretched away to the horizon. Sky and water were a uniform, monotonous grey. Not for the first time, Mrs Harvey wondered why the elderly flocked to Berthing-on-Sea.

The foyer of the Alexandra Hotel was abnormally crowded for a weekday in December. There were a great many middle-aged men with briefcases. Two of them were sitting at Mrs Harvey's usual table, the one near the radiator in the bow window. Miss Pope was not there.

Mrs Harvey peered at her watch and repressed a twinge of irritation. So like Miss Pope to be late.

'Mrs Harvey! What are you doing here?'

She recognized the voice rather than the face; her eyesight was not what it was. Joan, the fair, plump waitress, was carrying a tray laden with dirty crockery. She sounded harassed.

'I'm always here on Thursdays,' Mrs Harvey pointed out.

'But today's Wednesday.'

It took a few seconds for the information to sink in. Mrs

Harvey was not altogether surprised. One consequence of age was that time became elastic: it stretched and contracted unexpectedly.

'I think I'll have a pot of tea and some toast, nevertheless.' Mrs Harvey knew this was an indulgence for which she had not budgeted; but she needed time to recuperate before she faced the outside world again.

Joan shepherded her across to the window table. 'Bit of a rush today, I'm afraid, dear. Most of these gentlemen came for the auction at Warton Castle.'

Mrs Harvey disliked sharing a table with strangers, but there was no alternative. As she waited for her tea, she stared out of the window. The two men were examining some coins in small transparent envelopes. Her attention strayed to their conversation; short of covering her ears she could hardly avoid eavesdropping.

'I'd exchange the guinea for the Exeter half-crown and the 1723 shilling.' The thickset man at the far end of the table prodded two of the envelopes with his forefinger. 'How about it?'

NQOCD, Mrs Harvey thought: not quite our class, dear. The judgement was wholly out of place in these egalitarian days. No one was supposed to think about class any more.

'Don't be ridiculous, Newley,' the older man said. 'It's not as if the guinea was in good condition. Look at those scratches on the obverse. And the detail is very worn.'

Ex-army, Mrs Harvey decided. It had something to do with the carrying voice and the neatness of the clothes; he was the sort of man who kept his handkerchief in his sleeve.

'In that case, Fowler-Troon, there's nothing more to say.' Newley slipped the guinea into his waistcoat pocket. 'The shilling doesn't really interest me. I don't collect Hanoverians.'

Fowler-Troon swept the remaining coins across the table cloth. His elbow knocked his cup. Tea flooded towards Mrs Harvey.

'I'm so sorry.' He dabbed at the cloth with a handkerchief which he took from his sleeve. 'Clumsy of me. I hope you weren't splashed.'

'Not at all,' Mrs Harvey said. 'Coin collecting — such an

interesting hobby.' The little accident had flustered her, and she scarcely knew what she was saying. 'Did you buy them at the Warton Castle sale?'

'Eh? Yes. Rather a waste of time, actually. An American dealer got most of the good pieces.'

'So sad.' Mrs Harvey recovered her poise. She was glad to have an opportunity to talk to someone; it would give her something to think about afterwards. 'These country-house sales, I mean. An entire home going under the hammer.'

'Quite so.' Fowler-Troon refolded the damp, stained hand-kerchief and looked doubtfully at it. 'From my point of view, they're rather like lucky dips.'

'Unlucky, in most cases,' Newley said.

'I do like guineas,' Mrs Harvey said wildly, seeking to prolong the conversation. 'They sound so much more romantic than pounds. I've got a guinea at home. My mother used to say it was very rare.'

'What period?' Newley asked.

'One of the Jameses, I think. James III? There's some connection with Bonnie Prince Charlie, too.'

Newley snorted. His exasperation took Mrs Harvey by surprise.

'It can't be James III, I'm afraid,' Fowler-Troon said. 'We've only had two Jameses, unless you count the Old Pretender. He called himself James III, but of course he was never in any position to mint coins.'

'I believe my maternal grandfather bought it in Florence as a young man. Perhaps it was James II. I haven't looked at it for years.' Mrs Harvey frowned as she tried to remember. 'I've a feeling that the date on it was the same as our old telephone number — 1744.'

'That would make it George II.' Fowler-Troon looked at his watch. 'I must go if I'm to catch my train.'

'I'm sure it wasn't a George. Perhaps I'm getting muddled about the date.'

As Fowler-Troon was making his farewells, Joan arrived with Mrs Harvey's tea. Newley poured himself another cup and asked Joan for a slice of chocolate cake.

7

'You say your grandfather bought it,' he said when they were alone. 'When would that be? Sometime in the last century?'

'In the 1850s, I think. He travelled in Italy then, as a very young man. My mother said he bought it from an Italian who had once been employed by the Countess of something. It was a British title, I remember that.'

Newley's dark brows drew together. 'Not the Countess of Albany?'

'I think that was the name,' Mrs Harvey said; she was genuinely pleased for him. 'How clever of you.'

'That might give it curiosity value,' Newley said. 'She was the wife of Bonnie Prince Charlie.'

'How romantic.'

'It wasn't.' Newley gave her an unexpected smile which briefly transformed his sullen features. 'They fought like cat and dog. I think they were legally separated in the end.'

Mrs Harvey winced. 'What a pity.'

'Still, maybe your guinea's a sort of Jacobite relic. Tell you what: if you like I'll have a look at it for you — give you a valuation. You never know, it might be worth a small fortune.'

'Oh, I'd never sell it,' Mrs Harvey said firmly. 'Not after it's been handed down, all those years. It should go to my nephew. If he doesn't want it, I shall leave it to the nation.'

'But of course,' Newley said gently, 'it may not be worth anything at all.'

Mrs Harvey conceded that she had been wrong about Mr Newley. The rough diamond, she told herself, had a heart of gold.

He insisted on paying for her tea. He escorted her back to the flat. It was a rare pleasure to have a man's arm to lean on: one didn't have to worry about muggers, or the risk of a fall.

Once they were home, Mrs Harvey had a moment of panic, largely because her small, crowded sitting-room emphasized the bulk of her guest. Asking a complete stranger into her home suddenly seemed the height of folly. On the other hand, she told herself, the Alexandra Hotel was not a likely haunt for criminals.

8

As it turned out, his behaviour gave her no cause for concern. It took some time to find the guinea. It was literally years since she had seen it. Mrs Harvey's failing eyesight made the search more difficult. Fortunately Mr Newley helped her look for it.

It was he who discovered it in the theoretically secret drawer of the bureau, buried beneath paper-clips and rusting pen-nibs and wrapped in a yellowing envelope. The envelope was marked *Father's Guinea* in dear Mama's upright hand.

Mr Newley took the envelope to the window and shook the coin on to his palm. He studied it for what seemed like minutes.

Mrs Harvey could bear the excitement no longer. 'Well?'

He turned back to her. 'I'm sorry, Mrs Harvey. James II — 1686, with the elephant and castle below the bust.'

He handed the guinea to her. It lay, warm and golden, in her hand. The details were a blur.

'It is worth a few quid, even though the condition's no more than fair.'

'I . . . I did think it was James III.'

Newley shrugged. 'Easy to make a mistake. I mean, the coin's worn, and you're not an expert. Of course it may well have Jacobite associations. That would increase its value. If I were you, I'd look for something to support its provenance — letters, diaries, that sort of thing.'

'I'm so sorry,' Mrs Harvey said. 'I've brought you here on a wild-goose chase.'

'Never mind, Mrs Harvey. It's always a pleasure to look at coins.'

Chapter 1

THE FIRST DEATH occurred on the first Monday of the New Year.

Afterwards, however, Celia Prentisse looked back on the previous Saturday evening as the real watershed. In retrospect at least, it was then that an invisible curtain had descended, separating the precarious normality of the past from the dangerous uncertainties of the future.

Six of them had been sitting round the oval table. By the end of the meal, all of them had eaten too much without really noticing what they were eating. Celia was later to learn that each of the others had something to conceal, ranging from the embarrassing to the criminal. The secrets would cost two of them their lives.

'If you'll excuse me,' Georgina Newley said. 'I'll just . . .'

'Through the hall and on your left.' Arabella Lorton smiled, inviting sympathy. 'You have to pull the chain twice. Rod hasn't fixed it yet.'

Georgina's eyebrows quivered. 'I see. Don't bother to get up.'

Since none of the men had shown any inclination to do so, the last remark was not so much an indulgence as a rebuke. Georgina strode out of the room. As she closed the door, the atmosphere lightened perceptibly. Celia found Mrs Newley difficult enough at work; socially she was impossible.

'Have some Stilton.' Rod Lorton pushed the cheese-board towards Ivor Newley, who shook his head.

'There's more claret,' Arabella said. 'Darling, would you?'

Lorton picked up the bottle and looked enquiringly round the table. No one wanted any more except William Dougal. Celia wished he wouldn't drink so much, not that it was any of her business. Lorton spilt a few drops of wine on the polished mahogany of the table. He mopped it up with his napkin. For an instant Arabella's smile slipped.

'Do you specialize in any particular period?' William asked.

Newley glanced at him and looked away. 'The Stuarts.'

It was an unusually laconic reply. Newley rarely declined an opportunity to talk about coins.

'That's interesting,' William said amiably. 'Numismatically, I mean.'

'Why's that?' Arabella asked, ably seconding William's effort to revive the conversation.

He smiled at her, and Celia felt the familiar stab of jealousy. 'The Civil War produced a lot of oddities. Then there was the Commonwealth. And in Charles II's reign they stopped hammering coins by hand and started using machines. What were they called?'

'You mean the mill and screw presses,' Newley said reluctantly. 'It wasn't quite as simple as that.'

His thick-featured face was almost grim. Newley wasn't a man who had much time for smiling, but he could make himself pleasant enough when he chose. Celia wondered what was bothering him tonight; it was unlikely to be the office, because the firm had recently acquired two new accounts. He had been in a good enough mood yesterday. Georgina must have said something again.

Arabella turned to William. Her thick, straw-coloured hair glinted in the light from the silk shade which hung over the table. Celia didn't envy her looks: Arabella had that unattainable beauty you usually saw only in two dimensions, on the screen or in a magazine. But it was unjustly allied to charm as well. Celia hoped William would be proof against the combination.

'Aren't you doing something on the Stuarts?'

Arabella's words were innocent enough, but the way she said them contrived to cast an invisible web of intimacy across the table.

William seemed perfectly happy to be snared. 'Not the ones that minted coins. I'm doing some background research for a TV documentary on the Stuarts in exile. Bonnie Prince Charlie and that lot.'

Celia pushed back her chair, averting her eyes from William's face. Why did he have to stare at Arabella? You could drown in her eyes.

'Shall I put the kettle on?'

Arabella transferred the charm to Celia. 'Please. I'll bring the plates.'

Lorton, Newley and William sprang up to help Arabella. Celia told herself it meant nothing: she wasn't jealous; she just wished William wouldn't make a fool of himself.

She went into the hall. The lavatory was empty. Georgina Newley was standing in the doorway of the next room, which Arabella used as a combination of office and studio. She had switched on the light.

Georgina turned towards Celia. She showed no sign of embarrassment.

'So this is where it all happens,' she said; there was an odd note of triumph in her voice. 'It must be wonderful to be as talented as Arabella. So versatile.'

A dog whined in the kitchen.

'I didn't know they had a dog.' Georgina raised her bushy eyebrows. 'It is a dog, isn't it?'

Celia nodded. 'It's not theirs. They're looking after next door's spaniel for the weekend.'

'Really?'

Georgina swept into the dining-room; the stiff folds of her dress rustled as she moved. *Nosy old bag*, Celia thought. *She never misses an opportunity to poke around*.

In the kitchen Celia plugged in the kettle and shook the beans into the coffee grinder. The spaniel nosed around her ankles, depositing golden hairs on her tights. Celia diverted his attention with a piece of cheese.

She knew the Lortons' kitchen almost as well as her own. Rod and Arabella had moved into the house six months ago. At that time the basement flat, where Celia now lived, was uninhabitable; she had camped in the Lortons' spare bedroom until the damp-proof course, the replastering and the painting were finished.

Sharing the house was an arrangement which suited all of

them. Rod and Arabella needed a lodger to help with the mortgage; Celia needed somewhere to live. She had known Arabella for years: they had grown up in the same small East Anglian town, gone to the same school and been invited to the same parties. When Arabella moved to London, in her late teens, their friendship had dwindled to the ritual exchange of Christmas cards. But it had swiftly developed again since Celia came to London, a little over a year ago. Celia privately thought that they no longer had much in common; but old friendships could be extraordinarily resilient, perhaps because they had fewer illusions than new ones.

Arabella's husband had come as a surprise. Rod Lorton was a squat, powerful man, a widower and ex-soldier who now worked for a public relations company. He was in his early forties, nearly fifteen years older than Arabella. 'I'm the Beauty,' she had said when she first introduced him to Celia; 'he's the Beast.'

There were raised voices in the hall: Arabella was disclaiming any need for a male escort to the kitchen. A few seconds later she pushed open the door and came in with a tray.

'You angel,' she said vaguely to Celia. She began to stack plates and cutlery in the dish-washer. 'Sticky, isn't it?'

'It's had its moments,' Celia agreed. 'What's up with Ivor?'

Arabella shrugged. 'Too much of that woman, I should think. Thank God for your William. He's got Georgina reminiscing about her childhood. You know, when the villagers knew their place at the bottom of creation and there was always bloody honey for tea.'

Celia jabbed the spoon into the heap of ground coffee. Some of it spurted on to the work top. 'He's not my William. But I must admit, he's good with people like that.'

'Diplomatic.' Arabella closed the dishwasher with a bang. 'Just as well. Rod's about as diplomatic as a steamroller.'

'It can't be much fun for him, entertaining the boss and his wife.'

Arabella grinned. 'Not when the wife's Georgina. Which reminds me, she wants hot milk in her coffee.' She tossed back her hair. 'Pity we haven't any arsenic to go with it.'

*

'It was a very small world,' Georgina Newley said, 'but none the worse for that. Apart from the vicarage and the doctor's family we hardly saw anyone on a regular basis; socially, I mean. Of course by that time the manor was empty. But I'm sure I'm boring you.'

'Not at all,' William Dougal said. 'It's fascinating how much life has changed since 1939. It must have seemed such a stable world.'

Lorton thought: *You little creep.*

Newley lit a cigar. He was sitting on the far side of the room and had rebuffed Lorton's attempts to make conversation.

'It could have been the setting for a pre-war novel by Agatha Christie.' Georgina sighed majestically. 'Times have changed. We have a cottage in Hampshire now. The village seems to be full of commuters. Nobody has any roots, these days.'

The four of them had moved into the sitting-room. The smell of coffee drifted along the hall from the kitchen. Newley stared at the flames of the gas-powered log fire. Lorton was annoyed; but you could hardly tell your boss to snap out of it and stop sulking. It felt unbearably hot and the cigar smoke made his eyes smart.

'Rod!' Arabella shouted along the hall. 'Can you get the drinks?'

Lorton welcomed the chance of a change of scene. He went to fetch the glasses and bottles from the dining-room: brandy for himself, Newley and Arabella; Armagnac for William and Celia; and Cointreau for Georgina, who had a sweet tooth. He polished the glasses with unnecessary care, whistling softly under his breath. Anything to get away from the old trout and her memoirs. He could hear voices and laughter in the kitchen. Celia was the one guest tonight whose company he actually enjoyed.

It was the first time she had turned up with this particular young man. Arabella had asked her to bring someone, to make up the numbers. Lorton thought Celia should be able to do better for herself than William Dougal. It turned your stomach to hear him playing the flatterer with Georgina; and he would have done the same for Ivor with those precious coins, if Ivor had let him.

It was difficult to work out the relationship between Dougal and Celia. Arabella said they had known each other since they were children, that their parents had been friends and that they had been sweet on each other ten or twelve years ago. Now they were meant to be just good friends, but Lorton had a suspicion that Dougal wanted to be rather closer to Celia than that. He had a brief but satisfying fantasy which began with Celia asking him to stop the little tyke from pestering her.

Lorton had little time for most of Arabella's friends; he thought them flashy and brittle. He categorized them in his mind as 'Ya-Yas' — which was the term he had coined for people with affected voices who habitually mangled the word 'yes'.

But Celia wasn't a Ya-Ya. She reminded him of Sue, his first wife, though he had never mentioned this to Arabella. The resemblance was not physical — Sue had been small and dark, while Celia was fair and taller than Lorton. But both of them were reserved, determined and vulnerable; both of them expected the world to live up to the impossibly high standards they set for it.

His liking had nothing to do with sex, though he found Celia attractive; but no woman could hope to compete successfully with Arabella on that score. It sprang from the fact that Celia, like Sue, made him feel protective; and protecting Celia went some way — not far, but a little — towards expiating the guilt he still felt for failing to protect Sue. That was the trouble with a Catholic upbringing. You never got away from guilt.

Arabella didn't need protecting. It was she who looked after him, a state of affairs which Lorton did not altogether relish. She had even persuaded Newley to take him on, despite his relative inexperience, at twice the salary of his last job, with a car thrown in. Sometimes Lorton felt he allowed her to make too many decisions.

This house was a case in point. She had insisted on having it, despite the expense, largely because it was within easy reach of Primrose Hill. She brushed aside Lorton's protests that they couldn't afford it. Arabella's earnings as a freelance photographer fluctuated wildly from month to month. Public relations wasn't exactly a haven of security: you could be out on your ear before you knew what was happening to you. The fact that he was probably a better account executive than Newley himself had nothing to do with it: Newley was a director; Lorton was just a hired hand.

Crockery rattled in the hall. The dining-room door opened.

'What *are* you doing in there, darling?'

'Wishing they'd all gone home.'

Lorton picked up the tray. As he passed Arabella in the doorway, she nestled against him; it was both an invitation and a promise. He bent to kiss her but she slipped away from him. At the sitting-room door she turned.

'Rod, did you remember the Cointreau for Georgina?'

He nodded.

Arabella grinned at him. Then she stuck out her tongue at the closed door, in the direction of Georgina's chair. 'I *loathe* that woman,' she whispered.

William Dougal took the Armagnac with relief. He had had ten minutes of Georgina Newley's undivided attention and he needed an anaesthetic. He was glad to see that Rod Lorton went in for generous measures.

Mrs Newley took her Cointreau. She sipped it and said, 'Yorick.'

For a moment Dougal thought this was a novel form of 'Cheers'.

Ivor Newley stirred in his chair. 'All right, I hadn't forgotten.' He looked at Celia. 'You don't mind if we talk a little shop, do you? Have you roughed out the press releases?'

'I did them this morning. I hope they're okay — as a client he's a little out of the usual.'

'Pop music,' Georgina said firmly, 'is a product which someone manufactures. We get publicity for the person and the product. It's precisely the same as anything else.'

Celia flushed. 'Yes, of course. I only meant —'

'That the music press isn't our usual cup of tea,' Lorton said quickly. 'I know a bloke who used to work on the *Melody Maker*. If you like I'll ask him to check them out.'

Dougal's memory stirred. Yorick had had several chart successes five or six years ago. The songs were slick electronic jingles aimed at small girls on the fringe of puberty. Yorick himself had been an Identikit pop star who looked as if his appearance had been generated by a computer. Dougal sat up suddenly.

'Isn't he dead?'

Lorton shook his head. 'He had a few problems and retired for a while.'

The curt reply irritated Dougal. 'Drugs, wasn't it?' he said innocently. 'Heroin? And wasn't there something about an under-age girlfriend? Or was it a boyfriend?'

'Yorick has changed,' Georgina Newley snapped. 'He wants to leave the past behind, to build a new career as a serious musician. We have been retained to help him.'

'He's doing entirely different stuff now,' Celia said, 'and aiming at an older market. There's a new intellectual flavour to his music. Or so he tells me.'

'He looks different too.' Arabella dazzled Dougal with a smile. 'He's going in for leather plus-fours, uncombed hair and lots of stubble. I think he's modelling himself on the "Death of Chatterton".'

Newley leant forward, pointing his cigar at Arabella. 'The photo sessions went all right?'

'All except the last batch, the ones with the wind machine. I had to do those again, and I haven't had time to develop them, let alone mount them.'

'I'll need them by first thing on Tuesday at the latest.'

'You'll have them. Rod can bring them in on Monday morning.'

'There could be a lot of money involved,' Newley said. 'If Yorick really takes off we could expand into an entirely new sector of the business. Let's get this one right.'

Dougal sensed that there was something off-key in this little exhortation. Surely the agency was doing perfectly all right as it was? PR for the music business must be both specialized and chancy. The Newleys' enthusiasm was difficult to explain.

The conversation drifted away from him. The other five were all concerned with the agency; even Georgina was a shareholder and a director, though Celia said she rarely came to the office; her directorship was probably a form of tax avoidance.

They were discussing the details of the press conference which was to launch the reborn Yorick on the astonished world. It would immediately precede his comeback concert. Dougal thought of other things. Occasionally fragments of conversation intruded.

'I thought perhaps a Japanese motif for the catering. It seems appropriate. Just the food, of course . . .'

Dougal was looking at Celia. She was holding her own, even with Georgina Newley. The firelight flickered on her face. She glanced across the room to him, as if she felt his eyes on her. He smiled, and she looked away.

'Joe has *promised* me a good review,' she said to Newley, 'but if we're going to be sure . . .'

It was well over a year, now, Dougal thought: surely that was enough time?

Sixteen months ago, Celia's father had died. The shock jolted her out of a teaching job she loathed and an engagement which offered nothing except a modicum of financial security; it had driven her from Suffolk to London, and into a series of dead-end secretarial and tutoring jobs.

'The quality's a bit too grainy for my liking . . .'

At Lorton's suggestion the agency had taken on Celia as a secretary; she had been good enough to earn promotion to account executive. ('Some of our clients,' Newley had said, 'prefer to deal with a woman.') Now, thanks to Arabella, she had escaped from the world of grimy bedsitters masquerading as studio flats. Celia had made it, on her own terms. She was in a position to say no if she wanted to; if she said yes, Dougal would no longer have to feel that he might have forced her into a decision she might not want to make.

The spaniel scratched on the door. Lorton let him in.

'His name's Pumphrey,' Arabella said. 'Darling, isn't it time he went out? You know what happened last time.'

Dougal noticed that Lorton was grateful for an excuse to get away. No one, with the possible exception of himself, seemed to be enjoying this evening.

'We have an agreement,' Arabella said to no one in particular. 'Rod takes him out at night, and I take him in the morning.'

'Where do you go?' Dougal asked.

She turned the full force of her face on him. 'Primrose Hill. It's so convenient.'

Georgina tapped her husband on the shoulder. 'We really must go, dear. It's getting late.'

She stood up without waiting for a reply. Lorton hesitated by the door. Pumphrey nudged him with his nose.

'Must you really?' Arabella said. 'Have some more coffee first.'

Only Dougal saw Newley glancing at Georgina's broad back. For an instant Newley's heavy features were contorted. It might have been a spasm of indigestion. Either that or simple hatred.

Chapter 2

ONE OF THE attractions of Celia's new job was the Ford Escort which came with it. She sometimes felt that metropolitan existence had reduced itself to the pursuit and enjoyment of material possessions.

As a pattern for life, it had the merit of being both simple and quantifiable, like a motorway map of Britain with the distances marked between the exits. You always knew where you were. You never lost yourself in a tangle of unsignposted minor roads.

On Monday morning she drove to work, crawling through the thick stream of commuter traffic. It would have been quicker to have gone by underground, and she wasn't expecting to need the car at work today. But the overwhelming advantage of the car was that it allowed you a patch of comfortable privacy at the beginning of the day when you needed it most. Beyond the windscreen was a world of chapped faces and dirty snow. The tubes would be crowded with peevish, hurrying people in damp coats.

Inside the car she was warm, dry and entertained by Radio 3. You could almost forget you were in the trough of January. If she was going to sell out to Mammon, she might as well enjoy the perks.

The agency was always referred to as NCPR; no one seemed to know what the initials stood for. Its offices were on the sixth floor of an Edwardian building in Lower James Street. The building's façade had been designed to resemble a grandiose wedding-cake covered with ornately-moulded icing. The offices themselves had been sub-divided, refurbished and redecorated so often in the past eighty years that it was impossible to guess their original layout.

Celia edged the car into Bridle Lane. The agency's offices might be seedy, cramped and difficult to find, but at least you could park in the yard at the back of the building. Free and secure parking was the main reason why Newley continued to resist Georgina's pressure to move to a smarter location.

Entrance to the yard was by an electronically-controlled up-and-over gate in Bridle Lane, which ran parallel to Lower James Street. Celia rolled down her window and, ignoring the hooting from the delivery van behind her, fed her piece of plastic into the slot and punched in her number. The gate swung up and she drove through the narrow archway.

The yard was not an attractive place. Grimy brick walls surrounded it on all sides. Far above was a square of grey sky which pressed down like a lid. Black, cast-iron fire escapes zig-zagged to the ground, drawing the eyes down to the cracked asphalt and the bags of rubbish.

Newley's black BMW was already here. The other parking slots were empty. Celia locked the car and, tucking her briefcase under her arm, climbed slowly up one of the fire escapes. It was not a comfortable climb: the wind circled round her, prying out the crannies in her clothing; and the frozen snow on the treads made it unwise to move quickly. But the alternative — going through Bridle Lane and Brewer Street to the front entrance — would take much longer.

At least the door from the fire escape to the office was already unlocked; she wouldn't have to fumble with her keys and run the risk of dropping them again. She pulled open the heavy door and stumbled into the warmth beyond.

The door gave on to the open-plan section of the office which ran from the back to the front of the building. On the left were three offices which belonged to Newley, Rod Lorton and Hugo Brassard. Celia herself was not sufficiently senior to rate an office of her own: her desk was here, among the secretaries'. It was separated from theirs by a low partition; her status was further emphasized by an armchair in front of the desk and a sickly cheese plant behind it.

At the far end of the open-plan section was a small reception area for those who came up in the lift of by the stairs from the main entrance; the telephone switchboard was here. Directly to the right of the fire-escape door was a conference-room which was also used for the smaller presentations and product launches. There was a squalid little kitchen beside it. This, as Newley was fond of telling prospective clients, was where it all happened.

Little was happening now: it was still before nine o'clock. The door of Newley's office was closed. The only sign of life was the spider-like figure of Hugo Brassard who was leaning over Celia's desk as if it was a particularly large fly. When he saw Celia, he flushed and straightened up, his limbs twitching.

'I — um — I just wondered if you had the current *Campaign*. There's an article . . .'

Brassard fluttered away from her desk.

'I haven't seen it yet,' Celia said. 'I expect Rod's got it. Had a good weekend?'

She dumped her briefcase on the desk. Her top drawer was slightly open. Hugo had been poking around again. She suspected that he came in early precisely for that purpose.

At first the habit had exasperated her; now she tolerated it in the same way that you tolerated a friend's tendency to pick his nose in public. Brassard was interested in everyone's desk: he liked to know what was going on, to be able to nip mistakes in the bud.

'The weekend?' Brassard said wonderingly. 'Oh, I went down to Worthing. To see my mother.'

'She's well?'

Brassard pried because he worried. He was a partner in the agency, though the Newleys took most of the decisions without reference to him. He constantly anticipated bankruptcy or scandal at work, and ill health or burglary at home; he was also convinced that the country was about to be engulfed in revolution and that the world was on the brink of a nuclear holocaust. He might be right on all these counts, but his pessimism could be rather wearing.

'As well as can be expected.' Brassard shrugged his thin, high shoulders. 'It won't be long now, I'm afraid. Can I get you some coffee?'

'I'd love some.'

Brassard walked waveringly through the conference-room and disappeared into the kitchen. Celia hung up her coat and sat at her desk. She had come to respect Hugo, for all his quirks. For a start, he was good at his job. He handled the staider clients, the long-term bread-and-butter accounts which provided the agency with the bulk of its income.

These firms didn't require dramatic coups to bring them to the notice of the general public: they wanted a steady trickle of publicity in the places where it mattered for them. In most cases, this meant the trade press, where Brassard had excellent contacts. If one client, who made agricultural machinery, produced a new combine harvester, Brassard would write a glowing description of its qualities and ensure that the press release appeared, usually under someone else's name, in the professional farming journals. The client was pleased, especially when the article led to sales leads; the editor acquired some free copy; and Brassard had earned his fee.

Celia had her own reasons to be grateful to Brassard. It was he who had decided that the agency needed a woman account executive, and that she was the best person for the job. Lorton had backed the idea, but Brassard had done the real work of persuading the Newleys to agree.

She flicked open her diary. She would be in the office today. Tomorrow, she and Rod would be going up to Birmingham to hold the hands of one of their clients who had a stand at the National Exhibition Centre.

Brassard arrived with two mugs of coffee. He deposited one of them on her desk. 'You haven't forgotten the party?'

Celia shook her head. 'I'll ring the off-licence this morning to jog their memories. Zaza's going to do the food.'

Hugo screwed up his face. 'Is that wise? Couldn't you . . . ?'

She understood his anxiety. Zaza, their eighteen-year-old receptionist, had been chosen for her decorative qualities; Newley believed that the clients expected to see pretty girls around the place. Efficiency was not her forte.

'I'll keep an eye on her, Hugo, I promise. It'll all be very simple. She can't go far wrong on peanuts and bits of cheese, can she?'

24

'Nothing would surprise me in that department.' Brassard's eyes were on Celia's diary: he had probably trained himself to read upside down. 'And *please* make sure she gets receipts this time.'

The main phone began to ring. Brassard darted down the room to the reception area and seized the handset.

'NCPR.' he said sunnily. 'Good morning! Can I help you? . . . Mr Newley . . . Yes, he is in. One moment and I'll put you through . . . Hullo? . . . Hullo?'

Brassard put down the phone. 'Extraordinary,' he said to Celia. 'This chap asked if Ivor was here and, when I said he was, rang off. Just like that.'

'Perhaps he was called away.' Celia pulled out the Henry Magus file from her in-tray and opened it. Brassard hovered for a few seconds before disappearing into his own office.

Gradually the office filled up. Rod Lorton was the next to arrive. The secretaries straggled in, one by one. They moved like sleepwalkers through their early-morning ritual: visiting the loo, making coffee, opening the post and checking their in-trays. During coffee an animated discussion of the weekend's television developed. Celia kept her head down and wondered if she would hurt everyone's feelings if she invested in a pair of earplugs.

As usual, Zaza was the last to appear. She drifted into the office on a cloud of Chanel. She carried her coat on her arm; there was little point in putting it on because she was rarely exposed to the outside world for any length of time. Her father's Rolls-Royce ferried her between her parents' home in Bishops Avenue and the office.

Today she presented a tonal symphony of matching pinks. The other girls eyed her, expertly assessing the new wardrobe and its accessories. Celia beckoned her over.

'I've typed out a list for the party,' she said slowly. Everyone talked slowly to Zaza: it allowed time for the words to sink in. 'I want you to buy the stuff this morning; it shouldn't take long. Then you can lay everything out this afternoon.'

Zaza opened her large brown eyes to their fullest extent. 'Yes, Celia.'

'Hugo will give you some petty cash. And remember to get receipts this time.'

'Yes, Celia.'

The swing doors by the reception desk creaked as they opened. One of the secretaries gave a small, nervous giggle, instantly repressed. The visitor was a red-faced, elderly man; he was small, but compensated for this by giving the impression he was walking on tiptoe. He wore a pinstripe suit under his charcoal grey overcoat. The giggle was probably due to the bowler which he held in his gloved hand.

He slapped his free hand on the reception desk. 'Shop!'

There was another, louder giggle.

'Zaza,' Celia said. 'I think we have a visitor.'

Zaza swayed down the office. 'Hullo,' she said confidingly. 'Can I help you?'

The man stared past her. 'My name's Fowler-Troon. I want to see Ivor Newley.'

For once Zaza remembered her lines: 'Have you an appointment, sir?'

Fowler-Troon had found the nameplate on Newley's office door. 'No need. I'll announce myself.'

He strode down the room and opened Newley's door. 'Look here, Newley, I want an explanation.'

'This is a surprise,' Newley said. He made no attempt to disguise the sarcasm in his voice. 'Won't you sit down?'

'There's a word for people like you: unethical.' Fowler-Troon closed the door.

The outer office became unusually silent as everyone strained to hear the rest of the conversation. Brassard popped his head out of his room, saw Newley's closed door and withdrew.

Celia returned to the article she was writing on Henry Magus. She was meeting the features editor of *Tomorrow's Woman* for lunch on Wednesday, and was hoping to persuade her to take it. *Henry's psychic gifts first became evident at the tender age of three. At that time he was living with his parents and sisters in the East End of London. His grandmother, who had once worked as a maid at Buckingham Palace, lived with them. One day a fire broke out when the old lady was alone at home . . .*

The nice thing about Henry was that he actually believed he had saved his grandmother's life. Celia had jollied him into a three-month contract with the agency largely because of his sincerity. In his trade, sincerity was the next best thing to star quality.

She went to the filing-cabinet to verify the address where the astounding rescue had taken place. It was in the *Psychic News* article last month. Irrelevant detail always added a touch of verisimilitude.

Newley's door suddenly opened and Fowler-Troon emerged at speed. His skin was a darker red than before.

'I'm warning you, Newley,' he said over his shoulder. 'One more case like this and I'll have you blacklisted. No reputable dealer will take your money.'

He cannoned into Celia, tripped over her briefcase and would have fallen if she had not caught his arm.

'My dear young lady! I'm so sorry. Unpardonable of me.'

Newley's door closed with a bang.

'Don't worry,' Celia said. 'No harm done.'

He caught sight of the nameplate on Celia's desk and glanced up at her face. 'Prentisse? Any relation of Richard Prentisse? The historian?'

Celia nodded. Hearing his name on someone else's lips no longer made her stomach contract with sorrow. 'He was my father.'

'Met him in France. Nineteen forty-five,' Fowler-Troon said telegraphically. 'You've got his features, eh? Always read his books. Good stuff. Sorry to hear . . .' His voice tailed away; he fingered the knot of his tie. 'You work here? Yes, of course you do. Nice to have met you.'

He smiled stiffly at her and marched down the office, his eyes straight ahead and his head held high. The doors swung shut behind him and the chattering began.

Brassard popped his head out. 'That's him,' he said to Celia. 'The one who phoned. I'd better tell Ivor.'

Newley himself stalked out of his room. A cigar jutted out of his mouth at the Churchillian angle. He was jingling his car keys. 'Tell me what?'

'The — ah — the man who came. I think he phoned earlier. Wouldn't leave his name.'

'I see. Some bloody crank. I'm going out.'

Newley's secretary asked where he could be contacted. He ignored her and left by the fire escape door. A buzz of speculation broke out. Brassard retreated into his office. Celia frowned and tried to concentrate on Henry Magus. The next interruption came from Rod Lorton.

He paused by her desk. 'What was all that about?'

Celia shrugged. 'Someone called Fowler-Troon came to have a row with Ivor.'

'Work?'

'More personal, I think.' She decided it was none of her business to mention what she had overheard. 'Fowler-Troon said he'd known my father. It must have been in the army.'

Lorton grinned. 'You meet all sorts there — I should know.' He pulled on his coat. 'I'm going over to RTI: they want to check the releases for tomorrow.'

'Again?'

'They've thought of something else we should have added. You know, they've got their spreadsheets in a twist. It's the first time they've had a stand at NEC and they're terrified everyone else's will be better than theirs.'

The door closed behind him. Celia could hear him clattering down the fire escape. She turned back to Henry. *Doris Treadel of Dagenham testifies to his incredible powers as a medium. Shortly after her husband, Craig, had passed over, she asked Henry to try to contact him. Craig's will could not be found, though Doris knew he had made one. During the séance, which was held in the familiar setting of —*

'Well, where is everyone? Come on, girl. Cat got your tongue?'

Georgina Newley, shrouded in her enormous fur coat, towered over Zaza in the reception area. Zaza looked as if she was about to cry. She was not equipped to cope with the wives of managing directors.

'He's out, Mrs Newley.'

'Who's out?'

28

Celia put down her biro with a sigh and went to Zaza's rescue.

'Hello, Georgina. Ivor went out about ten minutes ago, he didn't say where. Rod's over at RTI. Hugo's in.'

'I see. I'll wait in Ivor's office.' She swept down the outer office, drawing Celia in her wake. 'Do you think one of these girls could bring me some coffee?'

'Of course.'

Georgina struggled out of her coat. It was an elderly mink which had begun to moult. Several used tissues fell from the sleeves to the carpet. Celia took it from her and hung it behind the door. She wondered what Georgina wanted: it was unusual for her to come to the office. Brassard appeared in the doorway.

'Oh. Georgina.' He blinked rapidly and tugged the lobe of his right ear. 'Sorry, I thought you were Ivor.'

One of the telephones on Newley's desk began to ring.

Georgina gestured to Celia. 'You'd better take it.'

Celia picked up the handset. It was Newley's private line, she noticed, which didn't come through the switchboard.

'NCPR,' she said brightly. 'Good morning.'

'Damn. Celia, is that you? It's Arabella. Is Ivor there?'

'He went out. Didn't say where. Can I take a message?'

There was a moment of silence on the line. Then Arabella laughed.

'Why not? Could you just say I've run into a hitch with the last batch of the Yorick prints? I'll drop them in this evening, after the party. Rod'll lend me his key.'

'Okay.'

Arabella rang off. Celia scribbled the message on Newley's pad, conscious that Georgina and Brassard were watching her. The line had been good, and they must have been able to hear both sides of the conversation.

'Cutting it rather fine, isn't she?' Georgina said.

'She'll manage.' Celia smiled. 'Arabella never misses a deadline.'

Georgina snorted. 'So I should think, with her charges. What time's the party?'

'Five-thirty,' Brassard said. 'It's just a small affair. Consumer clients, mainly, and a few journalists.' He shifted his weight on to one leg, which made him lopsided. 'We had the industrial ones before Christmas.'

'I know.' Georgina let the silence lengthen. Brassard tried the other leg. 'I was there. Where's that coffee?'

Brassard scuttled to the door. 'I'll find out.'

'Silly man.' Georgina settled herself in Newley's chair, thrusting her feet under the desk. 'I think it's about time we had some changes here. Don't you, Celia?'

Chapter 3

'*SEPPUKU!*' YORICK SEIZED the cheese knife and sliced it
across his stomach from left to right, prudently holding the
blade an inch away from his clothes. 'Then up. And out come
the bowels.'

'But isn't it a bit painful?' Zaza asked. She was standing
beside the table which served as a bar.

'And then a friend cuts off your head. He's called the
Kaishaku.'

'I still think it must hurt. If only for a little bit, before he cuts
off your head.'

Yorick brought his face close to hers and flared his nostrils.
'What is pain,' he asked gently, 'compared to the poetry of
honourable suicide? Through harakiri, man may be the equal
of the universe.' He widened his eyes which were lined with
kohl. 'He drinks the dark draught of death.'

'I think there's more vodka,' Zaza said. 'I'll see if I can find
it.'

Yorick turned away in disgust and bumped into Lorton. His
small green eyes flickered in recognition.

'I know you.' He made it sound as if he was conferring a
favour. 'You're Arabella's husband. Is she coming this evening?'

Lorton's hand tightened round the wine glass. 'No,' he said
evenly. 'Too much work on.'

Yorick jabbed the cheese knife into a chunk of cheddar.
'She's one of the few people who understands what I'm trying to
do in *Mishima*. I wanted her to meet Cyril. Cyril would make a
lovely *Kaishaku* for me. We could do a shot for the cover of the
album: you know, me on the dais with this great crowd of
upturned faces in front, and Cyril behind, sort of looming and
holding the sword; his face would be in shadow, of course.'

Lorton glanced across the conference room. Cyril was well over six foot, and broad to match. His head was shaven, and he had the sort of face which always looked better in shadow. He was wearing a cowboy outfit.

Yorick followed his eyes. 'It's white silk, you know. The boots and belt are Spanish. It's his birthday present. He's always had this thing about the Wild West. You'll never guess what it all cost.'

'No, I wouldn't.' Lorton edged between two cooing journalists and escaped to the far end of the table. *Honourable suicide.* Death was never honourable. A body was so much meat. The brat should go to a slaughterhouse and see the honour there. Sue's pale face rose in his mind. The eyes were open; there was a stain of dried vomit on the pillow beside her head.

'Rod! Nice to see you again.'

Eustace Tolby was standing in the doorway, showing a mouthful of yellow teeth. From the neck up, he looked like a sun-tanned goat. Above each ear was a wing of ragged, grey hair. His bald patch gleamed in the strip lighting.

'Good to see you, Eustace.' Lorton smiled with genuine pleasure: anyone was an improvement after Yorick. 'Let me get you a drink.'

Zaza gave Tolby a glass of Muscadet and one of her most winning smiles. He was her father's solicitor as well as Newley's.

'I hear you've been abroad,' Lorton said. 'Somewhere exotic by the look of it.'

'The Gambia,' Tolby said. 'Just a week. Jenny and I needed to recover from Christmas. All the grandchildren never stop talking. It's surprisingly cheap at this time of year. You should try it.'

'I'd love to. Trouble is, when I've got some free time, Arabella's booked up, and vice versa. That's the snag with working wives.'

'Yes, indeed.' Tolby looked away. 'Is Ivor about? I really wanted a word with him.'

Lorton led him into the main office, where Newley was making heavy weather of the managing director of RTI. Ivor was better with journalists than clients: with the former he could be his normal cynical self, whereas the latter demanded a hearty optimism which was foreign to his nature.

'Don't worry, Joe, I'll get them to itemize the expenses. It *is* a little more than usual, you're quite right.' Newley caught sight of Lorton and Tolby. 'Look, here's Rod. He can put you in the picture better than me.'

Joe clasped both hands round his tumbler of whisky. 'It's the expenses, Rod. Sixty-eight quid just sort of appeared, out of the blue. What I want to know is, what's it for?'

'I'll check it out with our accountant,' Lorton said smoothly. 'I wanted a word with you, in fact. Make sure you get a *Times* tomorrow. They're doing two columns on the exhibition, and RTI should be in the first paragraph. It's the graphics package that grabbed their fancy.'

Lorton nudged the client towards happier thoughts. It took little conscious effort. Soothing clients was a large part of his job. Dealing with their complaints took nearly as much time as getting them publicity. As he talked, he eavesdropped unintentionally on the conversation behind him.

'You got my note?' Tolby said. 'Pity about the timing.'

'The rumour's now confirmed,' Newley said quietly. 'Can you make dinner tonight? I'd appreciate it.'

'Of course.'

The two men were moving away, and Newley's next remark was inaudible. Joe was at first delighted by the news that RTI was getting national publicity; but it reminded him of the exhibition tomorrow, which brought on a severe attack of first-night nerves. Lorton coped conscientiously with this until a diversion arrived in the shape of Celia; she was accompanied by a small, plump man in a dark blue boiler-suit.

'Rod, Joe. I'd like you to meet Henry Magus.' She paused and added challengingly: 'The famous astrologer.'

'Delighted, I'm sure.' Joe glanced at the boiler-suit and then down at his empty glass. 'I'll just . . .' He slipped away to the bar where Zaza was distributing abnormally large drinks to a group of predatory males.

Henry clicked his tongue against the roof of his mouth. 'Not a happy aura, I'm afraid.' He smiled at Lorton. 'Yours is much better. Nice to meet you.'

They shook hands. To Lorton's surprise, Henry had a firm, cool grip.

'We're going to do well with Henry,' Celia said. 'It's in the stars.'

Henry laughed. 'Not just the stars. The Tarot confirms it, and so does the *I Ching*.'

Lorton smiled back, uncertain whether Henry was serious. At that moment they were distracted by raised voices in the reception area. Georgina Newley had arrived; behind her was the slight figure of William Dougal, half-hidden by her broad body.

'But the lamb's already in the oven,' she said loudly. 'You knew quite well that we were — '

Newley had to shout to make himself heard. 'I can't help that. I'm having dinner with Eustace. We've got things to discuss.'

Georgina pursed her mouth and made a sound like a pressure cooker letting off steam. She turned abrutly, bumping into Dougal, and marched out of the office. Newley swore. Everyone else pretended they had been doing something other than listening to the quarrel.

Dougal passed them on the way to the bar. He nodded at Lorton, who pretended not to see him, and smiled at Celia. Lorton noticed how Celia's eyes followed him across the room.

By now the party was thinning out. Yorick's high, thin voice could be heard explaining the intricacies of the Japanese tea ceremony to Zaza. Celia sank down on a chair.

'I hate Mondays,' she said. 'When are you going to tell my fortune?'

'I'll do it now if you really want, dear. I've got the cards. I never travel without them. It's like doctors and their little black bags.'

Celia shook her head. 'I'd rather do it in private.'

Henry glanced sharply at her. He nodded. 'So right, dear. It's not a party trick, is it?'

Newley beckoned Lorton away. He wanted to discuss the travel arrangements for the Birmingham trip tomorrow. He talked so earnestly and with such a quantity of repetitive detail that Lorton wondered if he had had more whisky than usual. It was difficult to hear in any case, because Cyril had broken into song. '*Deutschland über Alles*', sung in a rumbling bass, thundered through the office.

Yorick giggled. 'Who's pisty-wisty again? *Naughty* Cyril!'

Cyril broke off and began to cry. He lurched across the room and knelt in front of Celia. 'You like me, don't you? You like my birthday suit? You must!'

The sight of a gigantic man behaving like an overexcited three-year-old had a stupefying effect on everyone except Yorick, who was presumably used to it. Cyril laid an immense hand on Celia's knee and squeezed.

'Can I sit on your lap?'

Lorton was already moving forward. He knew exactly what he was going to do; and it would probably hurt Cyril a great deal. Newley wouldn't like it: but to hell with that.

To Lorton's surprise, he discovered that someone else in the room had faster reactions. William Dougal slipped away from the bar. He seemed to trip: his glass tilted in his hand and a large quantity of red wine cascaded down Cyril's shirt front.

The big man's mouth fell open. Dougal seized his arm.

'I'm *so* sorry. How stupid of me. We'd better wash it out right away. Come on, there's a sink in the kitchen.'

Cyril staggered to his feet. With one arm draped over Dougal's shoulders, he wobbled through the conference room to the kitchen. The crowd parted to let them through.

Dougal was talking: 'If we wash it out right away, it shouldn't leave a stain. It'll dry very soon, because it's such nice, thin silk . . .'

Zaza closed the door of the kitchen behind them. It was made of plywood and did little to muffle the retching that followed. It occurred to Lorton that he might have underestimated William Dougal.

The trickle of departing guests became a flood. In five minutes most of them had gone. Yorick sat cross-legged on the carpet, explaining the religious significance of Noh drama to Zaza while he waited for Cyril.

Lorton had a headache. He disliked the endless socializing

which went with his job, and the way that people always felt obliged to get drunk when someone else was providing the liquor. Clients rarely realized that the bill for the alcohol they guzzled would eventually, and suitably disguised, find its way to them.

As the office emptied. it became harder to avoid the empty bottles, the dirty glasses, the cheese trodden into the carpet and the overflowing ashtrays. The knowledge that he might spend the rest of his working life in this environment, mixing with these people, suddenly seemed unbearably depressing. There were other ways of earning a living.

Apart from Yorick and Cyril, Henry was the last guest to leave. Newley insisted having a Tarot reading from him; the request was phrased in such a way that Henry could hardly refuse without being downright rude. Newley grew blunter and coarser when he was drunk. It was impossible to argue with him. Lorton had no intention of trying.

The two men spent a few minutes alone in Newley's office. When they came out, Newley's gloom had changed to a painful jocularity.

'Load of old cobblers, chum!' He clapped Henry on the shoulder; the little man reeled under the blow. 'Dark strangers and unexpected fortunes — I ask you. But you've got a nice line in patter, we can work on that: it's worth its weight in gold.'

Henry said nothing. He seemed anxious to get home. Lorton offered to fetch his coat. When he came back, Henry was talking to Celia by the open door of the lift.

'Well, I couldn't tell him the truth, could I?' He was whispering, but emotion had given his voice a shrill, carrying quality. The emotion in question, Lorton realized with a jolt of surprise, was shock or fear. 'It's never happened to me before.'

Celia looked politely sceptical. 'It's a difficult situation, I can see that.'

'I mean, what can you say? The man's walking around under a sentence of death.'

Lorton cleared his throat. Henry twitched and looked round. His chubby face had an unexpectedly furtive expression. He took the coat with a nod of thanks and skipped into the lift.

'Say what you like, dear,' Henry said to Celia. 'The Tarot never lies, not to me.' He smiled at them both and pressed the button for the ground floor. 'Bye for now.'

William Dougal realized that the evening had gone irretrievably wrong when he met Celia by the lift. If she had been a house she would have had the shutters over her windows.

They walked up to Beak Street and had an unmemorable meal in an Indian restaurant. Dougal tried to keep the conversation going, but the patches of silence grew longer. She was wearing what he thought of as her executive outfit: a navy-blue suit with a white silk shirt; her hair was scraped back from her face. The clothes made Dougal feel they were transacting business. In the end both of them gave the curry an attention it did not deserve.

Celia pushed aside her plate. 'Thanks for helping with Cyril.'

'He just needed redirecting.'

'But I wish you hadn't interfered.'

Dougal glanced at her. 'I'm sorry. Reflex action.'

She avoided his eyes. 'I could have dealt with him myself.'

'Of course.' Dougal put down his fork. 'I didn't mean to trespass.'

But the damage was done. He knew that she had suffered from a surfeit of overprotective males in the past; her father and her former fiancé had been the worst offenders. He blamed himself: he tended to forget that Celia had principles.

Dougal looked at his watch. 'We'd better get going. The film starts at half-past eight.'

'Would you mind if we didn't? I've got an early start tomorrow.' Celia yawned. 'I'm half-asleep as it is.'

He hid his disappointment. After they had paid the bill, they walked back together to the office car park. The agency's windows were in darkness. The Escort was the only car left.

Celia unlocked the driver's door. 'Get in. I'll give you a lift.'

Dougal shook his head. 'It'll be quicker by tube. Besides, it'd take you out of your way.'

She didn't insist. Nor did she offer him a lift to the tube station at Oxford Circus.

37

In the event, Dougal couldn't face the underground. It would get him home too soon. There was no reason to hurry. He walked back to Kilburn, pausing twice for a drink in pubs he had never visited before. A blister developed on his right heel. The pain was a welcome but ineffective distraction from the thoughts that circled his mind.

The facts were perfectly simple. He was making a fool of himself over Celia. He had turned an adolescent love affair into a grand romantic myth: eternal happiness awaited him if he could win the hand of the girl next door. But the girl wasn't a girl any more; she didn't live next door; and she showed no signs of wanting to give him her hand. He could hardly blame her for that. Why should she want to entangle herself with a feckless freelance researcher? If she knew the whole truth about the last few years, she would be even less enthusiastic. Celia had principles: that was part of the problem. His problem.

By the time Dougal got home he was drunk enough to know he would have a hangover in the morning, but not drunk enough to stop thinking or drinking. There was an old framed photograph of Celia in his bedroom. He put it in the waste-paper basket and told himself he had made progress.

The whisky bottle was at least a third full. He took this as a good omen: providence was tempering the wind to the shorn lamb. He poured himself a substantial nightcap. His eyes strayed back to the waste-paper basket. Celia was looking at him and the whisky turned sour on his tongue. He removed the photograph from its frame. An eighteen-year-old girl, whom he had once loved, smiled up at him; and the smile was part of history, like the girl.

He couldn't bear to tear her in half. He laid the photograph gently in the waste-paper basket. He made sure it was face down. His caution was unwise, for on the back he found a message: *All my love, Celia.*

The frame was worth keeping, Dougal thought. After all, it was silver, and he should be able to raise a pound or two on it.

At first Celia thought it was something she had heard in her dream.

As she slid towards waking, the sounds continued and she decided they were outside her head. She turned over and stretched out her arm. The Lortons had given her a double-bed. She wanted the warm reassurance of another body: she found a smooth and chilly expanse of sheet.

In her dream someone had been in bed with her. She thought it was William. The subconscious mind had neither modesty nor dignity. Worst of all, it produced morality plays while you slept, providing a stage on which your fears and lusts could posture to their hearts' content.

She wondered what William was like in bed — as a person, not as a lover. Did he snore or dribble? Did he have nightmares? Did he wake up when the person he was with had a nightmare? She would never know now. The subconscious mind should have realized this.

The sounds eluded definition, partly because they were never very loud. The elusiveness irritated Celia and gradually brought her fully awake. The noises came from above her head: a soft regular padding moved from side to side of the Lortons' sitting room; and there was also another, less frequent sound, like someone quietly tearing a piece of cloth.

The darkness seemed absolute. Her mind supplied the image of burglars: two masked men wearing striped vests and carrying jemmies. She glanced towards the clock, partly for reassurance because it was the only source of light in the room; the time was five past three. If there had been someone else in the bed, she could have woken him and mentioned the sounds. The thought that she was indulging in cowardly wishful thinking had the effect of converting her fears into angry curiosity.

Celia switched on her light, swung her legs out of bed and felt for her slippers. She wrapped her dressing gown around her and tiptoed over to the bedroom door. It opened without a squeak.

The flat had its own front door which gave on to the area at the front of the house. But a flight of stairs led to the upper floors. At the top of the flight was a half-glazed door which opened into the Lortons' hall. There was light on the other side of the glass.

Rod or Arabella must still be up. It was probably Arabella.

Rod was going to go to bed early because of the Birmingham trip tomorrow. Celia climbed the stairs; she was fully awake now and Arabella would almost certainly have a pot of tea on the go.

In the hall the sounds were louder. The sitting-room door was half open. Suddenly Lorton appeared in the doorway. His face was different from usual: it was as if the skull beneath the skin had changed its shape. His eyes were puffy and there was stubble on his chin.

'Are you all right?' Celia said. She wondered if he was drunk.

'Hope I didn't wake you,' Lorton said; he was having some trouble with his articulation. 'Have you heard the news?'

Celia shook her head. She had a premonition that burglars would have been infinitely better than this was going to be.

'It's Arabella.' Lorton scuffed the carpet with the toe of his shoe. 'She's dead.'

Chapter 4

JUST AS THERE had been before, there was a post-mortem, an inquest and a funeral.

The police were sympathetic but thorough. The thoroughness was part of their job but the sympathy came as a shock. The police had been unexpectedly kind last time too, but Lorton had forgotten that until now. Arabella's death compelled him to relive Sue's.

The sympathy of the police was professional like everything else about them. It could hardly be otherwise, for they hadn't known Arabella in life; and they came across death too often to be sentimental about it.

Lorton was grateful for the cups of sweet, milky tea, for the pauses between the questions and for the lifts home. They even took the trouble to ask him, before the results of the post-mortem came out at the inquest, whether he knew that Arabella had been two months pregnant. He said he did. He had always wanted a child.

Celia's sympathy was harder to take, because it was personal and clumsy from lack of practice. He guessed that she realized this, because she tried to be as unobtrusive as possible. He found meals waiting for him in the oven. One evening they went out to dinner together, but that was a failure because Arabella came too. At his request Celia disposed of Arabella's clothes. She ferried them in three car-loads to a charity shop on the other side of London. She also dealt with the undertaker.

The house was suddenly far too large for him. He wished it would contract to a single room. It was full of silences. Possessions became booby-traps concealing pitfalls of memory. More than once he considered moving out to a hotel. Inertia kept him at home.

He wanted the funeral to be as quiet as possible. Celia was there, and so were Arabella's parents — a grey couple, both twisted by arthritis, who had seen little of Arabella since she moved to London. The agency sent flowers but no one insisted on coming. He kept the Ya-Yas away by the simple expedient of ignoring their existence.

Lorton had only met Arabella's parents twice before, once at the wedding. He knew they disliked him: he was not the sort of man they had wished their daughter to marry; he spoke with the wrong kind of voice and had the wrong kind of job. The father made it obvious that he blamed Lorton for his daughter's death. The mother asked if he was quite sure that Arabella had wanted to be cremated.

First Sue; now Arabella. He accepted his responsibility for Sue's death; Arabella's was a freak of fate. Nevertheless he could not rid himself of the idea that the two deaths were connected: a cause had led to an effect.

On the face of it, the notion was absurd. Arabella had driven to the office on Monday night, with the portfolio of Yorick photographs. She parked in the yard, but didn't turn on the outside light, presumably because she was in a hurry and she knew the way so well. All the offices were empty, apart from the security man on duty by the front entrance. There were no other cars in the car park. The gate locked itself automatically behind her.

Twenty feet up the fire escape, she slipped on a patch of ice. The police believed that she had been impeded by the portfolio. She bounced down one flight and slithered under the handrail. She might well have survived the fall. It was the sheerest bad luck that the side of her head had crashed into the stanchion that guarded Newley's parking space. Her body had been found by the security man making his rounds at midnight. The portfolio and its contents were undamaged.

The accidental death of a freelance photographer earned a mention in some of the newspapers, largely because Arabella had been beautiful. Even in death she managed to stand out from the herd; Lorton knew that would have pleased her. No one had noticed Sue's death.

Ivor Newley had telephoned twice since Arabella died. On both occasions he asked if there was anything he could do and urged Lorton to take off as much time as he needed.

Celia told Lorton that the idea of moving offices had been mooted again. He knew this could not be attributed to a fastidious desire to spare his feelings. No one could afford to be fastidious in PR. No one could afford to be associated with death, either. Death was bad for business. Newley's kindness to him was no more than skin-deep. A body on the premises and a widower on the staff were embarrassments.

On the weekend after the funeral, Lorton realized he could put off what had to be done no longer. The air in the studio was chilly and stale from disuse. There was dust on the filing cabinet and a mug of grey tea on the desk. It had always been his wife's room. For an instant his adult beliefs crumbled: it seemed perfectly possible that she was watching him as he pried into the private places of her life. But he needed to know the truth because it affected how he felt about her death. He was to blame for this last irony as well.

He had never admitted to Arabella that he was sterile.

Celia doubted if she had ever worked so hard in her life.

On the Monday after the funeral, she had no time for a cup of coffee, let alone lunch, until the middle of the afternoon. Lorton's absence inevitably meant more work for everyone.

In professional terms it had been a good day. London's major independent radio station had agreed to use Henry on its panel of experts for a psychic phone-in. A nationwide chain of department stores was showing real interest in retailing a selection of RTI's leisure software. The *New Musical Express* had agreed to interview Yorick around the time of his comeback concert.

It was the dead time of the day. Newley and Brassard, both recovering from heavy lunches, were silently immured in their respective offices. The secretaries yawned as they typed. For once no one was chattering. Zaza wilted picturesquely over her desk.

Halfway through her cup of coffee, Celia's telephone rang. She swore under her breath and picked it up.

43

'Celia? It's William.'

Celia spilled some of the coffee over the letter she'd been drafting. Arabella's death had made the coolness between them seem childish but had done nothing to make her feel less awkward with him. Since then they had seen one another once, when William helped her dispose of Arabella's clothes.

'Hullo. How are you?' She wondered whether all the secretaries were listening, or just some of them.

'Look, I said I'd look out for a bookcase for your sitting-room. A friend of mine's getting rid of some rack shelving. He wants a fiver for about twenty feet of it. Are you interested?'

'Yes, I am.' Celia thought of the cartons of books which disfigured the sitting-room. They had been there so long that she hardly noticed them any more. 'And thanks for remembering.'

'I could put them up for you, if you like. On the understanding that they might fall down.'

Celia giggled. 'When do you want to do it?'

'This evening?' His voice sounded more relaxed than before. 'We could get a takeaway afterwards.'

'I'd like that.' Celia calculated the probable time of her arrival at home and added half an hour for a bath and a change of clothes. 'Seven-thirty?'

'Fine. See you then.'

She put down the phone and returned to her letter. Part of her mind ran ahead to the evening: the new jeans, probably, and the black sweatshirt; and she might as well wash her hair in the bath.

A few minutes later her concentration was broken by a little squeal from Zaza. Celia looked up. Lorton had just come into reception. He was unshaven and wore a heavy leather coat.

'I'm not a ghost,' he said to Zaza. He glanced down the office. Everyone except Celia avoided his eyes. Office etiquette did not cover eventualities like this.

Lorton went into Newley's office without knocking. He shut the door. Celia could hear their voices but she could not distinguish the words. The volume gradually rose. The typing faltered and stopped. It sounded as if the two men were quarrelling.

The door opened.

Newley said: 'You're sacked. I should have done it months ago.'

'I'm not sacked. I've resigned.'

Lorton slammed the door and went into his own office. He opened drawers and cupboards and swept some of their contents into an empty cardboard box. Celia followed him.

'Rod, what's happening?'

He didn't look up. 'Isn't it obvious?' He threw a pair of shoes into the box. 'The parting of the ways.'

Brassard coughed behind her. 'We're all a bit off-balance at present. Naturally. You most of all, of course. But even Ivor: I know he's taken this very much to heart. He values your work so highly.'

Lorton straightened up. 'Catch.' He threw a bunch of keys to Brassard, who missed them; they clattered against the wall and dropped to the carpet.

'Please, Rod, don't be hasty.' Brassard picked up the keys. 'Things often seem better after a good — '

'Stuff it, Hugo, will you? I know you mean well but just sod off. I'd sooner work for King Kong than that fat bastard in there.'

He picked up the cardboard box and brushed past Celia and Brassard. The outer office was silent. As the lift door closed behind him, the whispering began.

Newley came to the door of his office. 'Hugo, Celia: I'd like a word.'

His face was still flushed, and he was breathing heavily like a man who had run for a bus. He waved them to seats.

'You've probably gathered what's happened: Rod's leaving us, I'm glad to say. The man's quite unbalanced. I may as well tell you that he has a distinctly murky past. We've been sadly misled about him.'

Brassard coiled his fingers together. 'Are you sure this is wise? I mean, Rod brought in — '

'Georgina agrees with me entirely on this.' Newley's words were a verbal slap: Brassard flushed. 'Celia, you'll have to handle RTI by yourself, from now on. Hugo and I will share Rod's other commitments between us, at least for the time being.'

45

'I suppose,' Brassard said, 'Celia might as well move into Rod's office?'

Newley shook his head. 'Georgina will take that. She's planning to be more actively involved.'

Celia and Brassard carefully avoided each other's eyes. In the silence which followed Newley's announcement, Celia wondered who had misled him about Lorton's past. And what had he done?

'I want both of you to think about recruiting a successor.' Newley drummed his fingers on his blotter. 'We want a young bloke, someone with drive. I'm not having someone who thinks PR means sitting on their back sides and sipping gin-and-tonic. The right outlook's more important than experience. I don't want another bloody cowboy. I want someone who gets results.'

Celia resisted the temptation to point out that Lorton had got results; there was no point in wasting her ammunition.

Brassard said perhaps a journalist would be the ideal choice; they knew what life was like at the sharp end. The remark was intended and received as oblique flattery rather than as a serious suggestion.

Newley sucked in his cheeks. Celia suspected he was enjoying this little display of power. Maybe Rod had managed to get under his skin. Newley jabbed a thick forefinger at her, as if reproving her for rebellious thoughts.

'I've got a job for you. Can you go to meet someone after work? Potential consumer client: he's into all this organic rubbish. Bristol-based. Honey, biscuits, stuff like that. Georgina's got him interested.'

'I had got other plans,' Celia said.

'This is important,' Newley said brusquely. 'Will you or won't you?'

Celia shrugged. 'All right.'

She could always postpone William's visit until later in the evening. She wasn't ready to declare war on Newley. Not yet.

Afterwards it seemed the final straw that she wasn't able to get in touch with William. She rang the Kilburn flat five times. No one answered the phone.

*

46

Dougal travelled by bus to Primrose Hill. It was not an easy journey.

He had bundled together his tools and the shelves in a black plastic sack. The smaller items kept escaping from the sack and sliding round the bus. It was partly his own fault. The American who sold him the shelving had insisted on celebrating the deal with a couple of joints.

Lorton's house was in the maze of streets to the east of Primrose Hill. Dougal got there a little after seven-thirty. The basement windows were in darkness, though there was a light on the floor above. The white VW Polo which had belonged to Arabella was in the little driveway, but neither Lorton's car nor Celia's were parked outside.

Presumably she was working late. He had no desire to trail back to Kilburn; on the other hand, facing a recently bereaved widower wasn't an attractive prospect either. The best course of action, as so often in life's crises, would be to find a pub.

At this moment the bottom of the plastic sack gave way. Shelves, wall-bars, brackets, an electric drill, a screwdriver, wall-plugs and screws spilled on to the pavement with a metallic clatter. One end of a shelf landed with its full weight evenly distributed between Dougal's feet. The pain made him swear.

A sash window shot up.

'What the hell are you doing?' Lorton demanded.

'Sorry,' Dougal said. 'The bag exploded.'

'It's you, is it?'

The window closed with a bang. A minute later Lorton came out of the front door. He helped Dougal gather up his belongings. Dougal explained what had happened.

'You can come in, if you want.' Lorton's face was in shadow; the invitation was spoken casually, but somehow it sounded like a plea.

Dougal accepted. In the hall, Lorton paused.

'Fancy a drink before you start?'

The sitting-room was no longer the tidy and tasteful place which Dougal had seen on the evening of the dinner party. All the flat surfaces, from the carpet to the upright piano, were

47

covered with files, papers, prints and negatives. The room was cold, despite the fact that the pseudo-log fire was blazing away. There were real ashes in the grate. Lorton scooped a pile of photographs from one chair and a stack of bank statements from another.

'Help yourself.' He gestured towards a row of bottles on the mantelpiece. 'Full ones on the left of the clock; empties on the right. That's the house rule.'

'I'm not disturbing you?'

'I wouldn't have asked you in if you were.' Lorton sat down. 'Fix me a drink, will you? It's the glass on the end. Pink gin.'

Dougal had the same. Lorton might be drunk but he was concealing it very well; he walked steadily and spoke clearly, if a little more slowly than usual.

'I'm sorry about Arabella,' Dougal said. It seemed best to get the formal condolences over as soon as possible. 'I liked her.'

'Most men did.' Lorton swallowed a mouthful of his drink. 'To be honest, I don't know what I feel now. But I think I'm probably glad she's dead.'

His face twisted and he began to cry.

Part of Lorton remained detached from what was happening.

He knew he was crying and marvelled at the fact. They were real, unforced tears: he hadn't cried like this since he was a kid. Dougal sat there, sipping his drink but making no attempt at consolation. He watched Lorton calmly, but not unsympathetically. He might have been a policeman.

The sobs gradually lost their impetus and degenerated into snuffles. Dougal felt in his pocket and produced a wad of paper handkerchiefs which he laid on the arm of Lorton's chair. After a while, Lorton wiped his face and blew his nose. For a moment there was a comfortable silence between them. They might have been old friends, whose conversation had reached a natural breathing space.

'Do you mind if I smoke?' Dougal said.

Lorton shook his head. He wanted to talk: the pressure was almost physical in its intensity, like a need to urinate. The wine-stain on Cyril's shirt was suddenly as vivid as blood in his memory.

'I told Ivor Newley I was going to kill him.'

Dougal showed no sign of surprise. 'I wouldn't do that.'

'Why not? I was in the Paras once. It's easy enough.'

'I know it is. But if you've already told him, he'll be prepared. Even if you succeed, why spend the next twenty years in jail? He's not worth it.'

It was a practical argument, and Lorton respected it for that reason. Most people would have pretended they hadn't heard what he said; alternatively they would have either run away or given him a holier-than-thou homily on the sanctity of human life.

'Maybe less. It'd be a crime of passion. I've just found out he'd been screwing Arabella for years. She was carrying his baby.'

'How can you be sure it was his?'

'I'm sterile. Sue and I did tests. My first wife. We both wanted children. Arabella said she didn't, not now. I never told her.'

'Have you any evidence to prove it was Newley?'

'There was.' Lorton nodded at the fireplace. 'Photos, a few letters. I burned them. Why?'

'I was wondering about blackmail,' Dougal said innocently. 'Georgina seems to carry a lot of clout.'

The meeting with Jeremy Murgatroyd dragged on until eight o'clock.

Celia took him to a wine bar in Kingly Street. He was in his mid-twenties, she guessed. He was fresh-faced, personable and full of enthusiasm. He told her that his one ambition was to be a millionaire by the time he was thirty. She asked him what he would do then; and that was the only time she saw him at a loss for words.

The meeting was a success in that Celia achieved what Newley wanted. She gave Murgatroyd the standard spiel about the advantages of PR. He needed little persuading and insisted on buying a second bottle of wine to celebrate. Celia turned down his offer of what he called a night on the town.

By the time she got rid of him, she was slightly tipsy. She walked back to Lower James Street; she had left her briefcase in the office. She went in by the main entrance. Most people avoided the fire escape as if it was haunted.

To her surprise, the lights were on. Georgina was clearing out the room which had belonged to Lorton. Her haste to move in was vaguely distasteful: it was like climbing into a dead man's shoes before they were cold. The analogy was not a comforting one.

Georgina beckoned her in. 'How did it go, dear?'

'Fine. I think he's hooked. He said he'd ring Ivor tomorrow.'

'Splendid news. I'll tell Ivor when I get home.'

Georgina in a good mood was worse than Georgina in a rage. A dreadful benevolence oozed out of her like sweet-smelling poison gas. It was often directed towards Celia, for Georgina believed that Celia added social and intellectual tone to the agency. She introduced Celia to the better-educated among their clients as if she was unmasking a hidden battery: ' . . . Celia Prentisse. The historian's daughter, you know.'

Celia picked up her case. She turned to say good night.

Georgina pre-empted her. 'This room's in a terrible state. But it's hardly worth redecorating, is it? Not if we're moving.'

'I suppose not.'

'I'm sorry Rod had to go like this. But I'm sure it's for the best. Ivor told me everything.'

There was a faint but unmistakable stress on the last word. Celia frowned.

'You knew about his little fling, didn't you?' Georgina continued. 'With Arabella?'

Celia sat down suddenly, on the edge of her desk.

'No? Well, at least he was reasonably discreet. It's his time of life, poor boy. She led him on, of course. I think he's learned his lesson.'

'I had no idea. With *Arabella*?'

Georgina clicked her false teeth. 'We musn't speak ill of the dead. Keep it to yourself, dear. Oh, and that reminds me. I expect you'll be moving soon, won't you? It's about time you had your own flat. Well, Ivor and I have put our heads together. We think we may be able to give you a raise in a month or two. An extra couple of thousand, if all goes well. You'll have no trouble getting a mortgage.'

'That's very kind,' Celia said automatically. The implications of what she had heard bombarded her mind like hailstones. 'I must be off — I've a guest waiting. Goodnight.'

She was so anxious to get away that she used the fire escape. As she closed the door behind her, she saw Georgina watching her with a smile on her face.

Celia let herself into her flat and switched on the light. William must have tired of waiting and gone home. She didn't blame him; she just wished he was here. Arabella and her unborn baby were reduced to a heap of ash. There wasn't time to be proud.

She went into the sitting-room. The shelves and assorted tools were scattered on top of the cartons of books. The room looked even worse than before.

There were steps on the stairs from the hall. William stood in the doorway.

'What's up?'

'Nothing,' she said bitterly. 'I've probably got us another client. Rod's resigned or been sacked. Georgina says she'll give me a raise if I move out of this house and don't try to seduce Ivor like Arabella did. And I'm starving.'

William put his arms around her. She clung to him and suddenly they were kissing.

Chapter 5

THE SOUND OF the drill from the basement reached Lorton in the spare bedroom two floors above. He found he was fully clothed under the duvet. The curtains were bright with winter sunshine.

It was just after eleven o'clock. He swung his legs out of bed and stood up cautiously. So far, so good. On the landing the drilling was louder. He ignored it and went into the bathroom. Arabella's toothbrush was still in the mug above the basin. As he emptied his bladder he stared at his face in the shaving mirror.

He neither looked nor felt as awful as he deserved. His memory of yesterday evening was patchy: he had several pictures like still photographs in his mind but it was difficult to link them together.

The pictures resisted his efforts to shuffle them into chronological order. He remembered sitting on the bed while William Dougal drew the curtains. Dougal dropped planks and tools on the pavement: perhaps that happened earlier, right at the beginning. At some point there had been a pint-pot filled with water. He could also recall three aspirins making a triangle on the palm of Dougal's hand. The number had seemed significant at the time: Lorton's normal dose was two.

He did his teeth and took a long shower, first hot then cold. The water running down his body reminded him that he had cried last night. The tears had been for himself, for Arabella and for a child who would never be born. He was not ashamed of crying, which surprised him.

The strange conversation came back to him while he scraped three days' stubble from his face. At first he assumed that he had dreamed of discussing the pros and cons of murdering Ivor Newley with Dougal. Killing Newley still seemed desirable, if far-fetched, like becoming a millionaire or finding a cure for cancer. But it was surely unlikely that he had talked over the idea with someone who was little better than a stranger. He also remembered Dougal saying something about blackmail. The rest of the conversation suddenly fell into place. Dougal must have been humouring him. But he had sounded entirely serious, and what he had said made sense.

Lorton rinsed the lather from his skin and frowned at his clean-shaven face. He had talked too much yesterday, and not merely to Dougal. His threat to Newley must be all round the agency by now.

There were clean clothes in his wardrobe. Downstairs in the kitchen he found that Celia had done the washing up and left a fresh pint of milk and the morning's mail on the table. He made himself a cup of instant coffee and two slices of toast. While he ate he looked through the post. It sorted itself naturally into three piles: junk mail, bills and Ya-Ya letters of condolence. He tucked the bills behind the clock and swept the remainder of his correspondence into the bin.

The drill had stopped. He wondered where Dougal had spent the night. Celia's Escort wasn't parked outside.

He picked up his jacket and went down to the basement. He found Dougal in Celia's little sitting room; he was trying to persuade a shelf to lie flat on its brackets. The bedroom door was open: the bed was unmade and there were two mugs on the dressing table. Lorton looked critically at the shelving.

'You should have used a spirit level.'

Dougal grimaced. 'I did have one. It got broken when I dropped everything last night. Is it lunchtime yet?'

'I was thinking of going down the pub.' Lorton hadn't even thought of lunch. But he knew that he didn't want to spend the next few hours in his own company.

Dougal looked at the network of unparallel lines on the wall and winced. 'I think I need a break too.'

They walked up to the Washington on the corner of England's Lane. It was a fine January day. People were smiling at one another; the shops were busy. It was strange to think that none of them knew that Arabella was dead; her absence made no difference to their lives. Beside him, Dougal almost pranced along the pavement. He was unshaven and, perhaps by contrast, his eyes seemed a brighter blue than Lorton remembered.

Their first pints washed down the sandwiches. Dougal bought another round. Lorton won nearly two pounds from the fruit machine so they celebrated with a third pint.

'I shouldn't be doing this,' Dougal said. 'I was going to work this afternoon.'

'I doubt it.' Lorton flicked a fingernail against his glass. 'You're not really in the mood for work, are you? Celia?'

Dougal nodded.

'That's the beauty of working freelance,' Lorton said. 'You can pick and choose what you do and when you do it.'

Their eyes met for an instant. The alcohol had reproduced the curious intimacy of the night before. Lorton felt a brief nostalgia for his own freelance days.

'I was a mercenary for a time,' he said abruptly. 'No one knew, except Arabella. She must have told Ivor. He flung it in my face yesterday.'

Dougal lit a cigarette. 'He disapproved?'

'People do. Didn't you know? It's okay to be a professional soldier if you join the army of your own country. If you join someone else's, you must be some kind of sadist.'

'Unless it's the French Foreign Legion. That's romantic.'

'Most of the legionaries I knew made Callan seem like Father bloody Christmas.'

'Being a mercenary was perfectly respectable until national-ism came along,' Dougal said. 'I suppose fighting was seen as a glorified trade: you sold your skills. Did you do it for long?'

'Two or three years. Angola and the Lebanon mainly. They make you earn your money.'

'Why did you stop?'

'My first wife found out.' Lorton paused, aware he was talking too much. Then it occurred to him that there was no longer any reason to hide what had happened in the past; he had nothing left to lose. 'I'd told her I was doing contract construction work in the Middle East. But when I got back to England there was a picture in one of the papers.'

'She was upset?'

'She killed herself.'

'Oh Christ. I'm sorry.'

Lorton hadn't been to confession for 25 years, but he remembered how it felt. William Dougal made an unlikely priest. Maybe the listening had always been more important than the absolution.

Dougal played with his glass. 'What will you do now?'

'Sell the house. I need the money. Not that there'll be much left over once I've settled the mortgage. I might go abroad again. I don't know.'

'And Newley? Did you mean what you said last night?'

Lorton tried to laugh: it came out as a croak. 'I was drunk.'

Dougal smiled. 'I was only going to say, there'd be no point in blackmailing him. According to Celia, he's already told Georgina.' He glanced across the table and added quickly: 'Don't get me wrong, I know you weren't really thinking of that.'

'You don't like Newley either. Why not?'

'I don't like him or Georgina.' Dougal shrugged. 'They're the kind of people who walk through you if you get in their way. I wish Celia didn't have to work for them. If they were in a Victorian novel they'd grind the faces of the poor. Then fate would catch up with them and they'd become bankrupt alcoholics. In the last chapter they might be allowed to repent on their deathbeds.'

Lorton vaguely recalled having to read novels by Dickens at school. He had a vivid impression of slabs of grey, close-set print sandwiched between worn, red covers. It suddenly seemed important to keep the conversation as close as possible to something you might have read in an old book.

'There'd have to be a twist,' he said. 'And in that sort of story it'd have to be their own fault.'

Dougal nodded. 'A fatal weakness would be their downfall. A passion for gambling, maybe, or an illegitimate child.'

'Newley hasn't got any weaknesses, not now,' Lorton said harshly; the word *child* grated in his mind. Oddly enough, the knowledge that Newley had made Arabella pregnant was harder to bear than anything else. 'Except those damned coins he buys. He drools over them, like that miser. You know — Scrooge?'

'He wouldn't like to lose them,' Dougal said. 'Would he?'

'He'd go spare. He'd have the fuzz running round in circles.'

Lorton glanced at Dougal and wondered where the hell they were: in real life or in the middle of a tale that someone might have written but never had? Dougal raised his eyebrows and spread out his hands, palms upwards, as if conceding defeat.

'I'm not sure we'd want the police around. Not in this sort of Victorian novel.'

'Miss Prentisse? This is George Fowler-Troon.' The voice became louder, as if its owner had moved the phone closer to his mouth. 'Er, we met the other day. I don't know if you remember?'

'Of course I do,' Celia said warily. 'What can I do for you?'

'Well, I was wondering, if it wouldn't be too much of an imposition, if I might possibly buy you lunch.' Fowler-Troon cackled unexpectedly. 'Your father bought me lunch once. It was in Rouen, I think. Never had a chance to repay him.'

'Well, that's very kind.' Celia had intended to get a sandwich and eat it at her desk. But the sunshine outside beckoned her. After last night, work seemed a tedious irrelevance, a refuge which was no longer needed. Moreover, she was unashamedly curious about Fowler-Troon's interview with Newley. 'When had you in mind?'

'No time like the present. Could you manage today?'

Celia said that she could. Fowler-Troon suggested that they meet at Daudet's in Old Compton Street. The choice of venue implied that Fowler-Troon wasn't short of money. Celia knew it only by reputation. Newley occasionally went there with clients from whom he expected rich pickings.

She reached the restaurant at ten to one, precisely on time. It was on the first floor of what had once been a small eighteenth-century town-house. Fowler-Troon was already at a table laid for two by the window. He rose politely as the waiter ferried her across the room.

As a host, Fowler-Troon proved to be attentive to the point of fussiness. Everything had to be precisely right for his guest. Would she prefer to face the room or the window? Was her seat quite comfortable? A little sherry while they consulted the menu? Was she sure that she had no objection to Sancerre with the meal? Should they order a bottle of mineral water as well?

During lunch they talked mainly of Celia's father; she soon realized that Fowler-Troon had not known him well.

The old man asked about her job; in exchange he told her a little about himself. She gathered that he had spent most of his adult life in the army. He mentioned a wife and grandchildren. References to horses and to a flat in town suggested that he was spending his declining years in considerable financial comfort. Once or twice he began to say something, paused and then branched out to another subject which had no connection with the one before. It was almost as if he was working himself up to making a confession.

After the meal, the waiter cleared the table and brought them coffee. Celia leant back in her chair. She had eaten much more than she usually did at this time of day. What she really wanted now was a nap.

'I'm sure that was a better lunch than my father gave you in Rouen.'

Fowler-Troon had the grace to look embarrassed. 'I must admit I have an ulterior motive. Not that one was necessary, of course. Always a pleasure to entertain a charming young lady.' He fiddled with the handle of his cup. 'Oh dear. I don't quite know how to put this.'

Celia took pity on him. 'Is it something to do with Ivor Newley?'

'You guessed?' Fowler-Troon dabbed his mouth with his napkin. 'It's all rather delicate. I don't want to tell tales out of school. But you ought to know. I'm sure your father would have wanted me to tell you. You may not want to continue working there, in the circumstances. It's not a question of mere tittle-tattle, you see.'

'What isn't?'

'This business about the Jacobite Guinea.'

'I'm sorry: I don't follow you.'

'I'm afraid I've plunged you in at the deep end. Let me start at the beginning. I've known Newley for quite a while now. Not as a friend, I should add; it's just that we both collect seventeenth-century English coins. I suppose you could call us rivals. Perhaps that's not *quite* the right word . . .'

Fowler-Troon caught her eye and smiled apologetically, as if aware that he was stalling.

'Last December,' he continued in a lower voice, 'I ran across him at the Warton Castle sale in Sussex. I bought something he wanted, and he bought something I wanted. We had tea afterwards in a hotel in Berthing, but we failed to come to an agreement. We were sharing a table with an elderly lady, a Mrs Harvey. She said she had a James III guinea in her possession, an heirloom which had come down to her from her grand-father.'

'*James III?*' Celia said. 'You mean the Old Pretender? But the Jacobites didn't mint coins.'

'If it existed, I imagine this would have been what we call a pattern, an unofficial design for a coinage which was never minted. A Jacobite sympathizer might have had it struck, in France perhaps or Rome.' Fowler-Troon sighed. 'A Jacobite Guinea would have made a fascinating pendant to my collec-tion. It'd be museum quality. Imagine it: the bust of James III; the Stuart arms; and an eighteenth-century date.'

'And does it exist?'

Fowler-Troon sighed. 'That's the trouble. I just don't know. At the time we asked Mrs Harvey a few questions. It soon became clear that she might have got the date and the king wrong, that she hadn't seen the guinea for years, and so forth. In any case, the whole thing was intrinsically improbable. I had to go — I had a meeting in town and I didn't want to miss the train. But Newley stayed. I thought no more about it till the following week. I happened to be in Berthing again — cousin of mine lives there. We were having tea at the same hotel when Mrs Harvey came in, with another old dear. I said hello, and after a time she remembered who I was. Oddly enough, she had the guinea in her handbag. Newley had come home with her and valued it. She'd just taken it round to a local dealer to get his opinion confirmed. And of course it wasn't a Jacobite Guinea at all: James II, second bust, 1686.'

'You must have been disappointed.'

'Not disappointed,' Fowler-Troon said sharply. 'Downright shocked. I was pretty sure I'd seen that coin before, in that very hotel. Newley bought it at the Warton sale. I remember the obverse was badly scratched.'

'You're saying there really was a Jacobite Guinea? And that Ivor switched it for another, less valuable guinea?'

Fowler-Troon nodded. 'Perhaps not a Jacobite Guinea; but it must have been something worth having.'

'He's not that stupid,' Celia said. 'It'd be tantamount to theft.'

'Precisely, my dear. Some collectors become obsessive, you know. But he wasn't stupid, not by his standards. He just took a calculated risk on the spur of the moment. This isn't an isolated incident. He's been guilty of sharp practice in the past, though this is undoubtedly the worst example I've come across personally.'

'Personally?'

'Well, I have heard a rumour that he once bought some stolen coins; but mind you that's just a rumour. He didn't even bother to deny this Harvey business when I accused him. Of course he'd sue me for slander if I made the accusation publicly. I can't prove it, not in the legal sense.'

'Thank you for telling me. I don't quite know what I'm going to do about it.'

'There's not much one can do, my dear. But I'm glad to have it off my chest.' Fowler-Troon's eyelids drooped. 'Imagine it,' he said softly. 'A Jacobite Guinea.'

William Dougal loomed at the foot of the bed. He was carrying two glasses and wearing Celia's dressing-gown and a guilty expression.

'All right, I admit it. I had a cigarette in the kitchen.'

'I could smell it,' Celia said sleepily. 'Like I could smell the beer on your breath this evening. What did you and Rod talk about?'

'Victorian novels and soldiering and putting up shelves.'

William sat on the bed and handed her a glass.

'This is champagne.'

'It seemed appropriate.'

'The Newleys are having a cocktail party on Friday. Georgina wants you to come.'

'Oh God.'

'It's your own fault. You shouldn't have buttered her up when they had dinner here.'

'I was only trying to jolly her along.'

'Will you come?'

'I'd go almost anywhere with you.' William swung his legs on the bed and began to lick her ear with a champagne-cooled tongue. 'Talking about the Newleys,' he mumbled between licks, 'are you going to look for another job?'

Celia pulled away her head. 'I'd leave now if I could afford it. Hugo might be able to help. And if Rod sells this house I'll have to find somewhere else to live.'

'You can move in with me.'

She turned his head so she could see his profile. 'One day, maybe; but not yet.'

His hand burrowed under the duvet. He ran a finger up her bare leg. She shivered with a blend of remembered and anticipated pleasure.

'I've found another reason to leave NCPR. You remember Fowler-Troon? I had lunch with him today. *Will* you stop tickling me? He's a retired brigadier and one of Ivor's rivals where Stuart coins are concerned. He suspects that Ivor has a secret collection of stolen coins. And he's convinced that he pinched a Jacobite Guinea from a widow in Berthing.'

'A *what*?'

Celia explained. William took her through the whole story. She could see the attraction for him: a curiosity like a Jacobite Guinea would be an excellent visual addition to the documentary he was researching.

William took her empty glass and put it with his on the bedside table. The dressing gown fell to the carpet. They wriggled together.

'Will you come?'

'I hope so.'

'I don't mean that. To the Newleys' party.'

William pulled her on top of him. 'One thing so often leads to another.'

Lorton spent the evening drinking bottled Guinness and watching snooker on the television. Both activities had a numbing effect on his mind.

He was on the verge of going to bed when he heard footsteps in the hall. William Dougal was standing in the doorway. He was wearing a blue silk dressing gown of Celia's and carrying two glasses and a bottle.

'Champagne?'

'You celebrating something?' Lorton said sourly.

Dougal poured the wine and sat down. 'According to Celia, Newley may have two coin collections. One's all above board. The other one's been built up illegally.'

'Doesn't surprise me. But so what?'

'If the secret one was stolen, he could hardly go to the police.'

Lorton grinned. 'I like it.'

'The trouble is,' Dougal said thoughtfully, 'if it exists, he won't have it on show. So where does he keep it?'

Chapter 6

'WE'RE TAKING A box at the Coliseum tomorrow evening,'
Georgina Newley announced to Celia Prentisse and William
Dougal. '*Salome*. It should be such fun. Now you will come,
won't you?'

'I only wish I could,' William said. 'Unfortunately I've got a
meeting with Verrall — he's the man who's fronting the
documentary.'

'I see. But you can manage it, can't you, Celia?'

Celia smiled and said she could. For an instant she had been
tempted to get out of the invitation with a lie. But she had an
old-fashioned regard for the truth; and besides it was time that
she gave Strauss another chance.

'Ivor!' Georgina called across the crowded room. 'Celia can
come tomorrow but William can't.'

Newley pantomimed pleasure and regret. Since Arabella had
died, he had been remarkably docile with Georgina. Celia
found it unnerving.

'Poor little Goo-Goo can't come, can he?' Georgina informed
her dachshund. 'Still, he can guard the house for Mummy and
Daddy, can't he?'

The dachshund slunk out of the room. Celia felt slightly sick.
She loathed the way some childless people treated their pets as
surrogate children. Her loathing was partly due to the suspicion that, in a similar situation, she might do the same.

'We shall be formal, of course,' Georgina said reverting to her
usual manner. 'I feel very strongly that someone should set an
example. After all, there are occasions and occasions.'

She moved away to talk to Eustace Tolby who had come with
his wife, an elegant Asian woman.

'Do you think,' William asked, 'that *Salome* will be an
occasion or an occasion?'

'Probably both, if Georgina's got anything to do with it.'

He looked at his watch. 'Let's go and see the coins.'

The collection was arranged in Newley's study, off the drawing-room. The room contained two hard chairs, a desk and an upright piano. The coins were displayed in locked glass cases. The more valuable pieces were normally kept in a safe, Newley told them. He showed them around personally, introducing the coins as though they were friends. Each exhibit had a neatly typed label.

Newley thawed in the face of William's obvious interest. He discussed with mounting enthusiasm the siege coinage of Charles I.

'There's a fascinating variety of design, even of shape. Look at the Newark half-crown for example: a lozenge. Or that octagonal shilling from Pontefract.'

William bent down to examine it. 'That's interesting: Charles II, yet the date is 1648.'

'That's because — ' The telephone began to ring. 'Damn.'

Newley picked up the study extension. As he listened, his face went grey with shock. He rang off.

'That was the police. We've got to clear the house. A gas main's ruptured and they're afraid of an explosion. Will you tell everyone? I want to get the coins.'

He was already unlocking the cases. Celia went into the drawing-room and announced the news. The babble of conversation stopped. Georgina ran from the room, crying 'Goo-Goo! Goo-Goo!'

Her departure created a subdued panic. People elbowed past each other to the door. Their expressions were drained of personality which gave them the family resemblance possessed by a flock of sheep.

Celia tugged at William's hand. He didn't move. She glanced at him, noticing that he was staring back through the partly open door of the study.

'Come on, William.'

He smiled at her, took her arm and led her to the window. They were the first outside.

*

On the following night Dougal and Lorton decided against taking the car; the distance from Lorton's house to the Newleys' was only a few hundred yards. They would be less conspicuous if they walked.

The streets were still sprinkled with people. It was a little after nine o'clock. Lorton was carrying a bag over his shoulder and humming under his breath.

Dougal was silent. His nervousness had grown steadily all day. Tonight was the Rubicon; afterwards there would be no going back. He tried to bolster his courage by reciting the reasons for what he was doing: 90 per cent of them boiled down to a pressing need for money, so pressing that the bank was threatening to foreclose on his mortgage; the other 10 per cent was divided between the desire to do Lorton a good turn and the feeling that the Newleys deserved whatever fate could throw at them. His courage refused to be bolstered. It was all very well conceiving these things in the abstract; the problems emerged when you tried to put them into practice.

Lorton stopped humming. 'You've done this sort of thing before, haven't you?' he said softly.

'Not quite like this.'

'Does Celia know?'

'Of course she doesn't,' Dougal snapped. 'And I don't want her to.'

The very idea made him cringe inside. He promised himself that this would be the last time he strayed beyond the legally-permitted limits in life; he couldn't risk the loss of Celia. He knew her too well to think that she would allow affection to outweigh her sense of right and wrong. Sometimes he thought that her simplistic morality was part of the reason why he loved her. Perhaps alien was a more accurate word than simplistic.

The road was a cul-de-sac. Dougal regretted that it was empty of pedestrians and moving cars. He had no excuse for turning back. Even when he was trying to be a criminal, the low moral fibre shone through. As they reached the privet hedge fronting the Newleys' garden, he was fervently grateful to have a last-minute reprieve: the drawing-room curtains weren't thick enough to conceal the light behind them.

'It's all right,' Lorton said. 'I saw them leave, and their car's not back. Gloves.'

The pulled on the rubber gloves. Dougal felt like a surgeon at the start of an operation which was doomed to failure. Lorton opened the gate. Dougal followed him into the little garden. They walked silently along the side wall of the house. The concrete paths had been cleared of snow and ice. There was no need to talk. Both of them knew the layout of the house, and they had planned their movements in exhaustive detail.

The dining-room had a Victorian sash window which was loose in its frame. Lorton slid back the catch with a thin-bladed knife and raised the lower half. Dougal heard him sigh softly with relief. There had been a strong possibility that the Newleys would have turned the security locks as well. In that case they would have had to break the glass.

Lorton passed the bag to Dougal and balanced himself on the sill, with his legs outside the house. Dougal held on to him. Goo-Goo began to bark; his claws rattled on the dining-room door.

Before he joined NCPR Lorton had worked in the personnel department of a firm which marketed burglar alarms. He reached down to the floor and folded back the carpet. Despite the cold, Dougal was sweating under his coat. Lorton hooked a leg over and climbed into the room. He turned back to Dougal.

'Come in slowly. I'll keep your feet away from the pressure pad.'

According to Lorton, the Newleys' burglar-alarm system was ten or fifteen years old and long overdue for retirement. Dougal wished he could share his confidence.

The reflections from the street lamps gave them just enough light to see what they were doing. Dougal took an old newspaper and a bowl from the bag. He laid out the newspaper on the carpet and stripped off the bowl's clingfilm covering. It contained a pound of raw stewing steak, laced with Seconal for good measure. Goo-Goo's greed was legendary, and he was reputed to be a messy eater. *Let sleeping dogs lie.*

Lorton opened the door, and the dachshund rushed in, yapping furiously. Dougal caught his collar and rammed his head into the meat. The transformation from faithful guard-dog to quivering glutton was almost instantaneous.

Lorton said: 'I still think it would have been better to kill him.'

'*No!*' Dougal hissed.

They went through the hall and into the drawing-room. A single standard lamp was alight. The door to the study was ajar.

Dougal was in front now. He had used an old trick last night —adapted from Conan Doyle's 'A Scandal in Bohemia'. Lorton's phone call had succeeded perfectly, rather to Dougal's surprise. It remained to be seen whether Newley, like Irene Adler, had realized the purpose of the hoax.

He ignored both the display cases and the safe which was concealed behind a framed eighteenth-century engraving of the City of London. Lorton helped him push the piano away from the wall. Dougal rolled back the carpet. Last night the piano had blocked his view, but he knew roughly where to look. He ran his hand over the parquet flooring until he found the area he wanted. Lorton passed him the knife. Dougal levered up the rectangle of hardwood.

The small japanned box was still there. He lifted it out and replaced the block of wood. The box was reassuringly heavy. Lorton, who had been watching anxiously, gave him a nod of approval.

They restored the carpet and the piano to their original positions. In the dining-room, Goo-Goo was just finishing his unexpected supper. He was too full to make more than a token protest when Lorton removed the bowl and rolled up the newspaper.

A few seconds later, they were walking down the road. The whole operation had taken no more than a few minutes.

'Who says crime doesn't pay?' Lorton muttered.

Dougal didn't answer. Crime has its expenses too. He was still trembling.

*

Lorton put the box on the kitchen table and attacked the lock with an old chisel. Dougal threw away the newspaper and washed up the bowl.

The lock was not designed for rough treatment. The lid flew up. Lorton emptied the contents on to the table. Dougal dried his hands and lit a cigarette.

There were about thirty coins arranged in layers on cardboard trays; each tray was encased in a plastic wallet. Beneath the coins were some papers.

Dougal bent down for a closer look. 'We really need Seaby's *Standard Catalogue of British Coins* for this. I think that's a James I half-angel . . . that's a William-and-Mary half-guinea . . . God knows what that is . . . there's a rarity, an Edward VIII threepence; out of period but who cares? . . . *ah*!' He pointed at a gold coin. 'Fowler-Troon was right. It's the Jacobite Guinea.'

Lorton looked sharply at him. 'I knew the bastard was bent.'

Dougal shrugged. At that moment they both heard the bang of the basement's front door. Celia was back from the opera. Lorton swept the coins together and crammed them into the box.

'Come on,' he said. 'We'd better put this away.'

Dougal picked up the papers and followed Lorton upstairs. They went into the spare room and sat on the bed. Dougal unfolded one of the papers and quickly handed it to Lorton.

Darling — Just a note to say I love you and I'm so glad. Always your Bella.

Lorton leafed through the rest of the bundle, wondering if the hurt and humiliation would ever stop. All but one of the letters were in Arabella's handwriting. Most of them were short and crammed with endearments. Phrases leapt up and hit him with a force which was almost physical. *I told Rod I was tired last night. I couldn't bear him fumbling over me after yesterday . . . The test is positive. I'm sure the baby's yours. They say women always know . . .*

He picked up the last letter.

Dear Ivor,

    I tried to ring you before the taxi came. I'll try again from the airport, but this note will have to do if I can't get through. I'm delighted by your news for your sake, and for Arabella's, of course. But for God's sake don't do anything impulsive. Divorce is complicated enough in normal circumstances. Yours are anything but normal, partly because of the baby and partly because Georgina's the major shareholder in the agency. And I imagine she's not a forgiving woman at the best of times. I'll be back from the Gambia on Monday, and we can talk this through in detail. Until then, I really would advise you to do nothing. Even seeing Arabella might be unwise. We also need to consider Rod's position.

All best wishes (to all three of you!)
Eustace.

He passed the solicitor's letter to Dougal, who glanced through it.

'That's another thing Newley will want back. Tolby's letter, I mean.'

Lorton dragged his mind away from his private misery. 'Why? Georgina already knows about the affair.'

'But she doesn't know that divorce was in the wind,' Dougal said. 'Nor the reason for it. It's a worse kind of betrayal. And she won't like the fact that Tolby's involved.'

'Nor do I,' Lorton snarled.

'Of course not.' Dougal paused. 'But it does give us a little more room for manoeuvre with Newley.'

'I don't want to manoeuvre. I want to kill him.'

When Celia got back from the opera, she was pleased to find the flat was empty. As she told herself several times, she was glad that she and William weren't living in one another's pockets.

William had said he might be late. He was meeting Gilbert Verrall, the presenter of a TV series called *The Footsteps of Time*. They had met originally when Verrall was writing a biography of Cromwell for which William had done much of the research. The projected documentary on the exiled Stuarts was Verrall's idea and he had commissioned William to do the spade-work.

It was just as well. William seemed to have no other source of income at present.

Celia had met Verrall once. He was a tall, well-groomed man in youthful middle age. He wore outsize glasses and talked excessively, usually about his work. William would be lucky to extricate himself before midnight.

She tidied up the sitting-room, promising herself an early night with a book. It was curious how soon you grew used to the presence of another person in your home. The flat seemed empty without William. She kept thinking of things she wanted to tell him. For example, if he had to smoke in her flat, he could at least have the decency to empty the ashtray.

The phone rang just as she had climbed into the bath. She wrapped a towel around her and ran to the sitting-room, swearing under her breath. Wet footprints trailed behind her.

'Celia? Thank God!'

'Who is it?'

'It's me.' The voice sounded annoyed by her question, as if instant recognition was no more than its due. 'Something terrible's happened. Cyril's gone.'

Yorick burst into tears. Celia asked where Cyril had gone. There were goose pimples on her arm. She tried to light the gas fire but dropped the matches all over the hearthrug.

'I don't know,' Yorick wailed. 'And I don't care. He just walked out with my best suitcases and half my wardrobe. I can't bear it, darling. You must come over.'

Celia ignored the last sentence. 'Did you have a row?'

'Cyril was very unkind to me.' Yorick sniffed. 'I let him read some of *The Journal of a Fallen Angel*, as a special treat. No one else has seen a *word*. And he said some horrid things about it.'

The Journal was one of Yorick's most cherished schemes. After his comeback as a serious musician, he planned to launch a book on the astonished and admiring world. It was to be a mixture of diary, autobiography, drawings and philosophical statement. Celia had spent part of last week trying to find a publisher who was remotely interested in discussing it.

'I'm sure he didn't mean to hurt you —'

'He did. He was a perfect little bitch. He called it a *wank*.'
Yorick, unmanned by the memory, began to cry again.

Celia managed to get a lighted match to the fire. 'Perhaps he's not capable of appreciating something like that.'

Yorick turned down this attempt at consolation. 'Oh Celia, I'm so unhappy I could kill myself. I wish he was here.'

'I'm sure he'll be back.'

'Please come round. I've been looking at the knives again. God, they're so tempting. I mean, why not? Nobody wants me. Nobody cares a damn.'

'We all care about you,' Celia said firmly. 'I think the book's going to be marvellous. Everyone who buys *Mishima* will want *Fallen Angel* as well.'

'No, they won't,' Yorick wailed. 'But I'll show them. I really will kill myself.'

Celia knew she had to take the threat seriously. Yorick had attempted suicide three times in the last four years; and the last attempt had nearly succeeded. She begrudged the sympathy he demanded from her; and she suspected that he was knowingly manipulating her. Still, she couldn't take chances.

'Now listen, Yorick, *I* care. I love you very much. I'll drive over right away. Just you hang on and I'll be there.'

'Oh Celia, thank God — '

Over the line she heard a door slam in Yorick's flat.

Yorick gasped. 'Cyril! *Darling*!'

There was a clatter as he dropped the handset. The endearments and other noises which followed made it quite clear that Yorick and Cyril were exploring to the full the dramatic possibilities of a reconciliation scene.

Celia hung up the phone. She warmed up the bath water. She lay in the bath, wondering when William would come home.

Chapter 7

LORTON WAS HAPPIER than he had been since Arabella died.

On the Tuesday morning he was whistling as he came out of the front door. Celia was trying to scrape the frost from the Escort's windscreen.

'I've got some de-icer,' Lorton said. 'Hang on, and I'll give you a hand.'

He fetched the can and the scraper from the Polo.

'How's office life?'

Celia wrinkled her nose. 'Grim. We're all supposed to be in mourning. Goo-Goo died in his sleep on Saturday night.'

'Ah well,' Lorton said. 'He was getting on a bit, wasn't he?'

It was a fine day, and Lorton enjoyed the drive to Hampshire. He kept the windows open because the car still smelled of Arabella's perfume. It seemed faintly sinful not to be at work on a weekday. He left the M3 before Basingstoke and drove south through Odiham. After a couple of miles he turned right into a network of lanes.

The Newleys' weekend cottage was called Miller's End. It was half a mile from the nearest village, which had become a haven for retired and commuting stockbrokers since the war. Georgina had invited Lorton and Arabella for a weekend last year. With hindsight, he thought it probable that Arabella had also been there alone, to meet Ivor.

The cottage itself was not exactly pretty: red-brick and four-square, it had been built for a farm labourer and his family in the middle of the last century. Georgina had smothered the interior with stripped-pine furniture and Laura Ashley fabrics in the early 1970s. Miller's End was as claustrophobic as a doll's house.

It was the only house on a single-track lane. Lorton followed the lane for another half mile, until it ended in a gravelled car park maintained by the National Trust. The Trust owned nearly a hundred acres, most of it along a low wooded ridge. A prehistoric version of the M3 followed the line of the ridge.

When Lorton had been here in the summer, the car park was nearly full. Families sat on the wooden benches squabbling over their picnics. The ridge had been alive with walkers.

In the middle of January, however, the place was desolate. Even the rubbish bins were empty. Tracks on the gravel suggested that the local kids used the car park as a skidpan.

Lorton locked the car and followed the path through the trees to the top of the ridge. Most of the snow had melted here. The path intersected with the trackway. This was wider than the path, and there were hoof-marks and fresh horse droppings.

He pressed onwards until he reached the clearing. It was about twenty yards in diameter. To one side stood a gazebo. Eight stone pillars supported a dome above a stone floor. Compass points had been carved into the circular slab in the centre of the floor. According to Georgina, it had been built before the woods were planted. Beyond the gazebo was a pond fringed with willows; dead leaves and beer cans floated on the surface of the water.

The floor of the gazebo was two feet above the level of the surrounding grass. Lorton scrambled up under the dome. As he remembered, a ledge of stone separated the rim of the dome from the tops of the pillars. Rusting wire-netting lined its upper surface, presumably to prevent birds from nesting there.

If he stood on tiptoe, he could reach the shelf. He gave the wire-netting an experimental prod: it moved easily.

Lorton took a Swan Vesta matchbox from his pocket and glanced down at the compass. He slipped the matchbox under the netting and pushed it back as far as it would go.

Only one more thing remained to be done. He jumped to the ground and continued along the path. It began to slope downwards. Lorton paused to consult his Ordnance Survey map. As a soldier he had been taught to err on the side of caution. It was always wise to work out a line of retreat as well as a line of approach.

*

On Wednesday afternoon, Dougal dialled the number of Newley's private office line. He had found the number in Celia's address book.

He was in the living-room of his own flat, sitting at the table he used for working. He wore a coat and a scarf because the electricity had been cut off at lunchtime. The lower two-thirds of his body was encased in a sleeping bag.

The ringing stopped.

'NCPR. Ivor Newley speaking.'

Dougal rested the transmitting end of the handset against the speaker of his battery-operated tape recorder. He pressed the play button.

'You lost several things on Saturday night, Newley, and you'd like to get them back.'

The voice was high-pitched, hollow and nasal at the same time. Dougal was pleased with it. He had experimented for hours in the tiled bathroom. He had finally chosen the version in which he spoke in a falsetto down a cardboard tube, with his nostrils clamped together.

'This is a recorded message, so all you have to do is listen.'

'What the hell is this?' Newley demanded. 'Some kind of joke?'

'First, if you don't agree to these very reasonable terms, certain documents will be made public. Several pieces of metal will be sold. In the circumstances they may have to be melted down.'

There was a wordless explosion on the other end of the line.

'These are the terms. You will obtain ten thousand pounds in cash. You will leave it in a carrier bag at a certain place and time. In exchange we will leave a coin for you, to show that we will keep our side of the bargain. The coin is dated 1744. When we are satisfied that this stage of the transaction has been completed in good faith, you will receive the rest of the items through the post.'

'Now wait a moment. Where — ?'

'You have until tomorrow to think about the proposition. If you agree to the terms, wear a hat whenever you are outside, even in the car. We will then contact you again about the time

73

and place. If you remain bareheaded we shall consider the proposition has been rejected and act accordingly.'

Dougal cut the connection, returned the handset to its rest and switched off the tape recorder. Almost immediately the telephone started to ring. He had a superstitious premonition that it would be Ivor Newley.

It was Celia. 'I hope I'm not interrupting your work.'

'No. I'd just come to a point.'

'Who are you on now?'

'Prince Charlie's younger brother — Henry, the Cardinal Duke of York. It's nice to think that the last of the Stuarts might have ended up as Pope.'

'So you're nearly finished?'

'More or less. After Henry I've only got the illegitimates and the collaterals. And Charlie's wife, the Countess of Albany.'

'I've remembered my excuse for ringing you. Are you coming to Yorick's concert on Friday? He made a point of asking. He says you're intellectual.'

'I wouldn't miss it for the world.'

'He's throwing a party afterwards, at his flat. About a hundred people have been invited, but I'm not sure how many of them will come. I mean Arthur Koestler's dead, isn't he? I'd better go. Ivor's in an even worse temper than usual this afternoon.'

On Thursday morning, Lorton mingled with the crowds in Regent Street. He didn't have long to wait because Newley was a man of habit and arrived at the office at much the same time, day after day.

The BMW was held up by the set of traffic lights just before Brewer Street. Georgina was in the passenger seat. Newley was wearing a flat cap made of tweed.

Lorton strolled away to a shop which sold office equipment. He told the assistant that he was considering buying an electronic typewriter. He asked if he could try one out.

The assistant introduced him to a demonstration model and left him to get on with it. Lorton typed: *This Sunday at Miller's End.*

Lorton removed the paper and left the shop. He went through the same process in another shop, where he typed: *Ledge in gazebo at WSW.*

He put the second letter in an envelope addressed to Newley at Miller's End. The first letter would be delivered by hand to Newley's house in Primrose Hill, early on Saturday morning. But he posted the second letter now, before he took the Bakerloo line to Kilburn.

Dougal shared the contents of the thermos between them.

'We have to see this through Newley's eyes,' he said patiently.

'Well, he can't go to the police, can he?' Lorton sipped his coffee and shuddered. It was lukewarm, black and very strong. 'Not without telling them about the coins. And he'd be forced to come clean to Georgina, as well.'

'Newley must realize that someone he knows is connected with the theft.' Dougal held up his gloved hand and ticked off the fingers. 'One, the thief knew the layout of his house and exactly what to take. Two, the thief knew the number of his unlisted private line. Three, the thief knew he never wears a hat. Four — '

'All right,' Lorton said irritably. 'And he'll think I'm the most likely person. But he can't prove it. He daren't even try.'

'If I were Newley, I'd want to know for certain, even if I intended to go through with the deal.'

'He will go through with it, don't you worry. Those coins are more important to him than anything.'

'He might hire a private detective to tail you. If nothing else, he'd want some sort of come-back if we cheated him after he handed over the money.'

'I never suggested that,' Lorton said. 'But it's not a bad idea.'

Dougal looked levelly at him. 'Newley may think it's a possibility. He may even wonder if he'll walk into an ambush on Sunday.'

Lorton sighed, blowing a plume of warm air into the room. 'You win. I'll stay at home with my alibi on Sunday, while you collect the money.'

Trusting Dougal not to do a bunk with ten thousand quid was insane. Then Lorton remembered that he had a hostage of sorts in the shape of the lodger in his basement. Dougal gave him a little nod, as if to say that he had remembered that too.

Yorick had wanted the Hammersmith Odeon for his comeback concert, followed by a nationwide tour of Britain's major cities.

Fortunately this was financially impossible. His manager, Simon, who was also Cyril's elder brother, had persuaded him to lower his sights — or rather to aim at a different and better target.

The target they chose was the Green Room, a club in Wardour Street. The club took its name from the colour of its walls, floor and ceiling. It consisted of a stage, a small open space which was referred to as the dance floor, and a bar selling a limited selection of alcoholic drinks in plastic beakers.

But the Green Room had a mysterious reputation for style. In the days when Carnaby Street had been the spiritual centre of swinging London, everyone went to the Green Room. The club was mentioned in the ghosted autobiographies of countless rock stars. A second cousin of the Queen had brawled on-stage with Manchester United's centre forward. A plain-clothes policeman attached to the drug squad had been accidentally electrocuted by a Fender Stratocaster, while trying to arrest the guitar's owner.

Even now, nostalgia gave the Green Room a certain news value. Simon knew that live music was not Yorick's forte, but he could hardly go wrong before a small and carefully chosen audience, especially if the bar prices were heavily subsidized: drinks were free for anyone equipped with a press card.

Simon and Celia had chosen the audience with great care. The majority of them were the surviving members of Yorick's fan club. Most of them were female and now in their late teens. Celia hoped they were still loyal enough to be decently enthusiastic, even if they found it difficult at first to appreciate the new subtlety of Yorick's music. The press was far and away the most important section of the audience. A number of celebrities had also been invited, chiefly to impress the journalists. Signed photographs, copies of *Mishima* and souvenir programmes were available.

Despite these preparations, the concert got off to a bad start. The celebrities had found other ways to occupy their Friday evenings. Yorick himself had an attack of stage-fright and emerged from his dressing-room half an hour behind schedule.

The band had been thrown together at the last moment; and none of the musicians looked or sounded as if he was enjoying the experience. The bass-player didn't turn up at all. The drummer turned up but was sick on-stage during the first number. After a twenty minute delay Cyril took his place but spent most of the time smiling at the audience. The keyboards player spilt beer on his synthesizer.

These technical hitches failed to disguise the quality of the music. Yorick had discarded the strong rhythms, the simple melodies and the accessible lyrics which characterized the first phase of his career. He recited dramatic monologues to a background of atonal noise.

His erstwhile fans did not appreciate experimental novelties. The first number earned a few scattered handclaps for old time's sake; the second was received with silence; after the third, a ten-minute dirge entitled 'When The Lotus Blossom Drops In My Tea', booing broke out. Midway through the fourth song, Yorick gave up and stumbled off the stage. One by one, the members of the band followed suit. Only Cyril remained, dribbling happily as he tapped the rhythm of 'Jingle Bells' on the snare drum.

Celia tried to salvage what she could, but she knew few of the journalists personally. Newley might have been useful here, but at the last moment he had decided not to come. Some of the journalists had already left; others had settled down to the serious business of getting drunk. She found William at the bar. He borrowed someone's press card and brought her a drink.

'This is disaster,' she muttered.

'You did your best. It's not your fault the music was so awful.'

'The whole thing's been jinxed. It might've helped if Ivor had bothered to be here.'

77

'Celia, dear!' Henry Magus bobbed up between Celia and Dougal. 'I've just seen Yorick: he's determined to go ahead with the party.'

'Oh God, when will it end?'

Yorick's flat was just off Church Row in Hampstead. It was a large, first-floor apartment which had been furnished as a suitable setting for an up-and-coming superstar. Four years later, the white carpets had turned grey; the leather-look upholstery no longer pretended to be anything other than plastic; and the electronic gadgetry had been sold.

The gathering was rather smaller than Yorick had envisaged. William Dougal counted eleven people, including himself and his host. Three of them claimed to be journalists but probably weren't. Mona, the solitary groupie, was in charge of refreshments. She had projecting teeth and told everyone who would listen that she had been in love with Yorick since she was twelve.

Cyril emptied several grams of cocaine on to a circular mirror and began to cut it up with a razor blade. Yorick drew his samurai sword and disembowelled a cushion.

'Ivor Newley, Ivor Newley,' he chanted. 'Kill, kill.'

'What's he got against Newley?' Dougal asked.

'He blames him for the press not being here,' Celia said. 'And Ivor promised he'd come tonight.'

Mona leant over the cocaine with a rolled-up five-pound note in her hand. She sneezed. The cocaine flew in all directions. Yorick hit her with the flat of his sword.

'Do you know a good solicitor?' Simon asked. 'I feel like suing somebody for all this.'

'The only solicitor I know is Eustace Tolby,' Celia said. 'Are you going to sue us?'

'I wouldn't recommend Tolby to anyone,' Henry said earnestly. He was slightly drunk and his face was pink.

Simon shrugged. 'I wish I could sue you. It beats cutting up cushions any day.'

Henry slipped away to the table where the bottles were kept.

Dougal followed him. 'I'm thinking of making my will,' he lied. 'I was going to ask Tolby about it. Do you think I shouldn't?'

Henry looked over his shoulder with theatrical caution. 'Not if you value integrity in your professional advisers.'

'What do you mean?'

'Have you ever heard of the Devenish case?'

Dougal shook his head.

'Devenish was a medium, and a good one too. But he prostituted his gift.' Henry pursed his lips. 'And that is a sin I can't forgive. He set himself up as a one-man cult. He specialized in elderly ladies. He persuaded seven of them to change their wills in his favour. The eighth one wasn't quite so credulous, so he forged her will and smothered her.'

'How does Tolby come into this?'

'This is confidential, you understand?' Henry stared appraisingly at Dougal. 'Tolby helped Devenish frame the new wills. He may even have had something to do with the forgery. His name didn't come out in court, but I knew one of the women involved. She's dead now.'

'Why wasn't he struck off the Roll, or whatever they do to solicitors?'

Henry shrugged. 'There was no proof. Devenish didn't betray him. I don't know why. Perhaps Tolby had something else on Devenish. Our Eustace isn't a fool: he'd make sure he was covered. If he heard this conversation he could throw a writ for slander at me.'

'You seem very certain,' Dougal said. 'But have you any real evidence against him?'

Henry drew himself up to his full height of five-foot-three. 'There is more than one kind of evidence.' He tapped Dougal on the chest. 'Believe me, William, sin and crime leave their marks on the soul's face. A true psychic can always see them.'

Dougal looked away.

Chapter 8

CELIA WAS WORRIED about William.

On Sunday he seemed unable to settle. He wandered round her flat, answering her attempts at conversation with monosyllables. In desperation she dragged him out for a stroll on the Heath. He walked fast, with his head down, taking little notice of where they were going.

It was lunchtime, so she suggested having a drink in the Flask. William agreed with an uncharacteristic lack of enthusiasm. Even more unusually, he ordered tonic water.

'Look, what's wrong?' she asked when they got back home. 'And don't say nothing.'

He lit yet another cigarette. 'I don't know. Hangover?'

'You tell me.'

'Would you mind if I go over to Kilburn? I'm not very good company today. I might as well do some work.'

'Go wherever you like,' Celia said. She went into the bedroom and made the bed with unnecessary violence.

When William had gone, she thought of all the things she had planned to do as soon as she had a little time to herself. There were letters to write, clothes to wash, and the cooker to clean. She could watch television or go to sleep. It was fortunate that she and William had such a flexible relationship: they could do as they pleased, and not necessarily together; each of them was still an individual.

She chose the cooker and began to scrape its insides with wire wool. While she worked she wondered what had really been wrong with William. The better you knew someone, the more you realized you didn't know.

A series of thuds brought her to her feet. Glass shattered. The floor shuddered beneath her. She ran into the sitting-room.

The rack shelving, together with its load of books and ornaments, had finally given up its unequal struggle with the force of gravity.

Dougal spent the rest of the day with the Countess of Albany.

After her separation from Bonnie Prince Charlie in 1784, she eventually settled in Florence with her tame poet, Alfieri, who possibly became her second husband. He died in 1803. She continued to live in her house on the Lung'Arno, patronizing scientists and literary figures, and holding nightly receptions at which she expected to be treated with the etiquette due to reigning royalty. At the same time she received a pension of £1,600 a year from the privy purse of her late husband's rival, George III of Great Britain. She was clearly a lady who knew how to make the most of life.

The phone rang at last. It was after six o'clock. Dougal reached for it so quickly that he knocked over one of his candles.

'He's back,' Lorton said. 'You can go now.'

'Any other activity?'

Lorton chuckled. 'Tolby came over this afternoon. Just happened to be passing, you know the sort of thing.'

'You think Newley checked back with him before he went to the cottage?'

'What do you think?'

Dougal absently relit the candle from the stump of the other. He had spilt wax over a reproduction of Fabre's portrait of the Countess. Now the time had come, he felt weak and light-headed, as if he hadn't eaten for days. The future had become the present. It smothered him like dense mist. Never again would he be so stupid as to embroil himself in something like this.

'William? You still there?'

'Yes. I . . . I knocked over a candle.'

'Well, then. On your bike.'

The car, a ten-year-old Ford Capri, belonged to Dougal's dope-smoking neighbour upstairs. Dougal had arranged to hire it for the Sunday and the Monday, just to be on the safe side.

Lorton had put up the cash. They decided that in the circumstances it would be foolish to bother about insurance.

Driving through London in a strange car, even on a Sunday evening, would normally have been a terrifying prospect. Dougal believed that cars were unpredictable creatures at the best of times. Tonight, however, the lesser worry was obliterated by the greater. He was vaguely aware that he was driving rather better than usual. He even managed to overtake another car.

For once his map-reading was flawless. He had a bad moment between Chiswick and Richmond when a police car stayed on his tail for half a mile. At Sunbury he reached the M3 and accelerated to a reckless 50 m.p.h. The car heater kept him warmer than he had been since leaving Celia's flat. Perhaps everything was going to be all right, after all.

He switched on the radio and learned that temperatures of minus 6 were expected tonight; the forecaster believed they were due for a 'cold snap' which could last at least a week. Dougal thought of his unheated flat and shuddered.

Once he left the M3, his little store of optimism rapidly evaporated. Three times he had to pull over to examine the map. It seemed to bear the same relationship to the country he was travelling through as Ptolemy's view of the world to a satellite picture of the earth.

There was little traffic on the roads. After Dougal turned off the A32 there was even less. He made a series of false casts, wondering at the apparent inability of the Hampshire County Council to conceive and implement an efficient system of signposts. It was with some relief that he found a village which actually admitted it was called Short Soham. Two miles beyond it, the Capri was negotiating the potholes of a poorly-maintained farm track.

By this stage Dougal was relying on Lorton's instructions. These were a more effective guide than the map or the Hampshire County Council. There was one bad moment, when he met a car going in the opposite direction. He hoped that the driver would remember nothing more than a pair of headlights.

The National Trust car park was empty. He switched off the engine, cut the lights and lit a cigarette. The darkness swirled around him. He was on the south-east side of the ridge; Miller's End and the other car park, which Lorton had used, lay to the north-west. Somewhere out there was the gazebo.

He willed himself to sit quietly, allowing his eyes gradually to adjust to the night. The sky was clear. The stars and a thin crescent moon shed just enough light to show where the path led up through the trees. It was a place of silence and shadows, an unnatural habitat for a city-dweller.

Dougal stubbed out the cigarette and checked his torch. Lorton had lent him a black Balaclava helmet which covered all of his head except the eyes and the bridge of the nose; feeling like a trainee terrorist, he pulled it on; he was grateful for its warmth. He picked up the canvas shoulder-bag, which was empty except for the map and a compass. His other item of equipment was a heavy iron-tipped walking-stick which he had brought for reassurance.

It was bitterly cold. The air chilled his lungs. The ground was already thick with frost which crunched beneath his feet as he walked. He forced himself to go slowly, with frequent pauses to listen. Now that he was outside the car, the night seemed full of noises.

It was darker among the trees. At intervals, splashes of light fell across the path, giving it a striped appearance. A small animal ran over one of the stripes, a yard in front of him; Dougal wondered which of them was the more terrified.

Something hard and metallic, concealed in the shadows, sliced into his leg. He bent double with the pain but managed to restrain himself from crying out. When the pain receded, he shaded the torch with his hand and switched it on: the rusting fragments of a disembowelled car were strewn in the bushes; he had barked his legs on the side of a door which protruded on to the path. People chose the strangest places to leave their rubbish.

He pressed on with even more caution. The path began to widen. A moment later he reached the clearing.

The gazebo made him suck in his breath. It squatted incongrously among the trees, looking like a visitor from another planet. The dome was silvered with frost. The interior was a nest of shadows. The surface of the pond beside it was smooth and dull with ice.

Dougal waited while he counted to a hundred. His eyes swept from side to side, probing the edges of the darkness. The cold seeped through his boots and socks and worked its way through his feet.

As he waited, he ran through the reasons why Newley was unlikely to have set up a trap. First, the man was miles away in London. Secondly, he needed to get back the coins and the letters without publicity which might reach his wife or the police. Thirdly, the Jacobite Guinea should have convinced him that the thief intended to keep his side of the bargain.

There remained a faint possibility that Newley would try to identify the person who collected the money. He would need a hired watcher for that, or a camera operated by remote control. Neither eventuality was likely. In any case, the darkness and the Balaclava cut down the risk of recognition.

Dougal stepped softly over the rough grass towards the gazebo. Nothing moved. He swung the stick in front of him, like a blind man searching for obstacles.

The low stone base of the gazebo felt comfortingly solid. The floor was dappled with pale moonlight, scarcely lighter than the shadows which mingled with it. He supported himself against a pillar with his free hand. He canted his body and raised one knee on to the floor of the gazebo. Just as he was about to lever the rest of himself up, a shock jolted through him.

In the patch of moonlight by the pillar was a human hand, splayed palm downwards on the flagstone like a monstrous silver spider.

Only five legs — can't be a spider.

It was a left hand. There was a plain wedding band on the third finger. The hand was not quite flat: it looked as if it was trying to get up. A dead leaf balanced precariously on the knuckles, twitching in the breeze.

Dougal's breath was coming in short gasps. His gloved hand

84

groped for the torch in his coat pocket. He shielded the thin beam as best he could; he felt it was like a beacon, alerting the whole county. By its light he connected the hand to the arm of a dark suede coat. Hunched against the base of the pillar was a round object, the size of a football, covered with short, wiry hair. The coat had huddled its contents together, as if trying to keep them warm against all odds. Two stumpy cylinders, covered with brown corduroy, dangled from the edge of the coat furthest from the head. The cylinders lay untidily, one on top of the other. Each of them ended in a shiny black shoe.

In moments of crisis the strangest reflexes determine action. The thought of his own danger dwindled to insignificance beside a wholly altruistic desire to help. Before he knew what he was doing, Dougal had scrambled into the gazebo and was kneeling beside the body. He supported the head with one hand and pulled the upper shoulder towards him. For an instant the jawbone touched the bare skin of his wrist, in the gap between the top of his glove and the cuff of his coat. The jawbone felt as cold as a joint of beef in a supermarket deep-freeze. The body flopped on to its back, nudging trustingly against Dougal's legs. He picked up the torch and turned it back on. The eyes and the mouth were open. Gold fillings studded the crooked teeth. The coat was unbuttoned. The body was no more than dead flesh.

When Dougal realized this, the strangest reflex of all briefly took control of him: his eyes filled with tears. He had seen death before but had never grown used to it. He was angry with it for existing, and terrified by the reminder that one day he might catch it himself. The impulse to cry disappeared as inexplicably as it had come.

He glanced at the head, which was resting in the crook of his right arm. A sour taste flooded into his mouth. For the first time, he allowed the features to assemble themselves into a face.

It belonged to Ivor Newley.

Dougal was halfway back to the car park before it occurred to him that flight was not necessarily the wisest course of action.

He pulled up and leant against a tree. His panting sounded abnormally loud. He forced his mind into action, though he was aware that a state of panic and a temperature around zero were not the best conditions for clarity of thought. He had made two blind assumptions: that Newley had been murdered; and that Lorton was somehow responsible.

It occurred to him that Newley might have died a perfectly natural death — a heart attack, perhaps, brought on by the blackmail. (There was no need to mince words now.) In that case, both the money and the Jacobite Guinea would still be in the gazebo; the police would infer from them that Newley had gone to the gazebo for more than just a Sunday stroll. God knew what their enquiries might unearth. In the unlikely event that someone other than Lorton had killed Newley, the murderer might have left behind both guinea and ransom for the simple reason that he didn't know they were there. Dougal realized he would have to go back and find out.

Surely Lorton wouldn't be so foolish as to kill Newley? He would be the obvious suspect. *But suppose Lorton had intended from the first to rob Newley, to murder him, and to present the police with a strong case against someone else?*

The idea had a ghastly plausibility about it. Dougal's stomach churned. He had come to like and trust Lorton; he had assumed that the feeling was reciprocated. But it was easy to put another interpretation on his behaviour. Lorton had not been exactly friendly before Arabella's death. His apparent change of heart afterwards might have been the result of calculation. Dougal, not Lorton, had been among the Newleys' guests when Newley had been tricked into revealing his hiding place. Celia had passed on Fowler-Troon's information about the secret coin collection to Dougal, not to Lorton. Lorton had insisted that they both took part in the burglary, when he could easily have done it by himself.

It was true that Dougal had suggested that he came alone tonight. But Lorton might have suggested it himself, if Dougal hadn't been stupid enough to volunteer.

He realized abruptly that there was no room for doubt: Lorton had condemned himself when he rang Dougal just after six to say that Newley was back in London. Between then and now there would not have been time for Newley to drive down to Miller's End, walk to the gazebo, get himself killed and become as cold as he was. There was only one explanation. Lorton had lied.

He walked slowly back to the clearing. If he was right, then Lorton's ingenuity might well have taken him one step further. An anonymous telephone call to the police must have been one option; but that seemed unlikely because in that case the police would already be here. A stronger possibility was that Lorton had left something which incriminated Dougal on or around the body, and was relying on the next passer-by to report the corpse to the police.

Nothing had changed in the gazebo. Dougal started with the body. The first thing he discovered was that Newley had not died accidentally. Three stab wounds made a neat triangular pattern on his chest. The wounds were shaped like pendants in silhouette: each slit was rounded and broad at one end, and tapered to a point at the other. One or more of the cuts must have found his heart. Dougal tried to distract himself from what he was doing by treating the wounds as a mental puzzle. He concluded that a single-bladed knife had been used; the blade was probably about an inch wide; Newley's assailant had stood in front of him; the slant of the stab wounds suggested that the assailant was right-handed, like 90 per cent of the human race.

Surely Sherlock Holmes could have done better than this?

Newley had been wearing a black, loosely knitted jersey, which was why Dougal had not noticed the wounds earlier. There had been little blood, which implied that Newley had died soon after the attack began.

The pockets held the usual impedimenta: two sets of house keys, a wallet, a handkerchief, a small penknife and a driving licence. The wallet contained an assortment of plastic cards and sixty pounds in notes. He was tempted to take the cash; but in the end he decided to leave well alone. Notes could be traced.

Dougal examined the floor of the gazebo, finding nothing except bird-droppings, sweet-wrappers and dead leaves. He checked the shelf above the pillars. As he had feared, there was no sign of the Jacobite Guinea or £10,000 in notes. Their absence strengthened the case against Lorton.

He jumped down to the grass and did his best to search the clearing. The futility of what he was trying to do swept over him. To be certain he would have to search the entire National Trust site. Why stop there? Lorton might have left something incriminating at Miller's End. He could search until dawn, or until the torch battery gave out, and still be in the same position.

The breaking point came when he reached the side of the gazebo. The pond stretched to within inches of the stone base. Dougal bent over to examine a scrap of paper. Just as he discovered it was yet another Mars Bar wrapper, he slipped and pitched forward.

In other circumstances it would have been comic. He swung his body round as he fell. He landed on the edge of the pond. His foot went through the ice as if it had been paper. He gasped as the boot filled with cold water.

He sat on the edge of the gazebo, wrung out the sock and dried himself as best he could. His teeth were chattering. He had had enough of searching. If only he could give himself more time. *Simple*, he thought sarcastically. *Just delay the discovery of the body.*

At that moment the idea hit him. He grabbed the walking stick and hobbled to the side of the pond. The ice was barely a quarter-inch thick. The tip of the walking stick plunged through it. Dougal forced it downwards, as nearly vertically as he could manage. Just before his gloved hand reached the water, the stick jarred on the bottom of the pond. At a conservative estimate the water was nearly a yard deep, even near the edge. He made two more soundings further along the bank and got the same result for both.

Temperatures tonight reaching minus six . . . A cold snap, lasting at least a week . . .

If he could weight Newley's body and roll it into the pond, the ice would seal it off for days; it might not be found for months, if no one dragged the pond. The time of death would be difficult to fix. If the body lay there for long enough, even the means of death could be hard to ascertain.

There was no time to think it over. Dougal grabbed the body's legs and hauled it on its back to the edge of the gazebo nearest the pond. Fortunately Newley had been wearing a tie and belt.

He made two journeys down the path to the wreckage of the car. The first time he returned with the door against which he had knocked his shin; on the second trip he fetched a dented wheel which had lost its tyre.

The wheel rim screeched against the stone but Dougal ignored it. Desperation had cancelled out his caution. He unbuckled the belt and, leaving it around Newley's waist, looped it through the wheel and through the glassless window of the door. It was just long enough. He knotted the end of the tie round the other side of the window. Then he shut his mind to the host of possible consequences and pushed.

The legs caught against one of the pillars. Dougal picked them up and used them as a lever. He thanked God that rigor mortis had not set in; presumably the cold had delayed it.

The body and its burdens teetered on the edge of the gazebo. Suddenly it passed the point of no return and plunged downwards. Dougal, taken by surprise, nearly toppled after it.

The splash sounded like an exploding bomb. Dougal cowered back, praying that no one would hear it. Water slapped against the base of the gazebo. He advanced cautiously and played the torch over the surface of the pond. Much of the ice had vanished. Waves careered from side to side. But there was no sign of Ivor Newley.

Dougal felt lightheaded, this time with relief. He picked up the bag and the stick. He shone the torch over the floor of the gazebo, checking he had left nothing behind. The beam picked out a small pale oblong by the pillar nearest the pond. Something had been trapped underneath the body.

The cold made his fingers clumsy. He put down the torch and used both hands to scoop up his last-minute discovery. It was a Midland Bank cheque book, three-quarters used. The torch beam dimmed perceptibly. The battery, like the torch's owner, was on its last legs. Dougal frowned at the cheque book and opened it. He sat back on his heels and swore. Nothing made sense.

The cheque book belonged to R. B. Lorton.

Chapter 9

CELIA ALMOST WELCOMED the idea of going to work. At least it would be a distraction.

According to the radio, it was the coldest January day for five years. There were icy patches on the roads, even in central London. She concentrated on her driving and wished she could stop thinking of William.

Last night she had swallowed her pride and rung the Kilburn flat twice. If he was there, he wasn't answering the phone. She promised herself that she would try once more when she got to work. If he didn't answer, that was his problem.

Unfortunately it was also hers. It was all very well to remind herself that she and William were individuals who gloried in their independence, and that he had said nothing about getting in touch or when he would be back. The unpalatable truth was that his absence hurt her. And it worried her too (*He might have had an accident — should I phone the police?*), almost as much as it angered her (*He might have had the decency to let me know he wouldn't be in to supper*). At the back of her mind was the thought that he might be with someone else. She knew so little about him. The possibility that he had another woman was even harder to bear.

She reached the office before eight-thirty. Newley's BMW and Brassard's Honda were already in their parking slots. She walked round to the main entrance and took the lift. Georgina Newley was conferring with Brassard in the reception area. The heating had been off over the weekend, and the office was like an ice-box.

'Look, here's Celia,' Hugo said unnecessarily. He twitched his shoulders as if shrugging the burden of Georgina on to the new arrival.

'I was just telling Hugo,' Georgina said. 'I'm terribly worried about Ivor. I haven't seen him since yesterday morning.'

'His car's outside,' Celia said.

'Of course it is. I used it myself this morning.' Georgina fished out a grubby paper handkerchief from the pocket of her mink coat. She blew her nose. 'You haven't seen him at all?'

Celia shook her head. 'What was he doing when you last saw him?'

'He said he was going to drive up to the Spaniard's for a drink. That was about midday. I heard him go.'

'In his car? Or yours?'

'His car. I found it last night, parked a couple of streets away.'

Brassard coughed. 'I don't suppose he could have gone down to Miller's End?'

'Without a car? Don't be silly, Hugo.'

'Sorry.'

'Have you tried Eustace Tolby?' Celia asked.

Georgina nodded. 'He hasn't seen him. I've telephoned everyone I can think of, but it's no use. Ivor's vanished. I just can't understand it.'

'Have you told the police?'

'Not yet. I thought perhaps — '

The phone on Zaza's desk began to ring. All three of them stared at it for an instant. Then the spell broke. Celia was the first to reach it.

'NCPR. Good morning.'

'Celia, it's me.'

'Oh . . . I see.'

'I'm sorry about yesterday. Can I come round this evening?'

Celia was convinced that Brassard and Georgina could hear everything. She kept her voice neutral. 'That would be fine.'

William chuckled unexpectedly. 'Witnesses, eh? I love you.'

She put down the phone and tried to wipe the smile from her face.

Georgina snorted. 'You know how we feel about personal calls at the office, Celia. Quite apart from anything else, it sets such a bad example.'

Dougal left the flat at nine o'clock. He had bundled everything he had worn yesterday into a couple of carrier-bags. There was no sense in taking chances.

He took the North London line to Acton and walked from there to Hammersmith. He scattered his clothes across West London in a variety of dustbins and builder's skips. He had hoped that walking would keep him warm. Life without a winter coat was going to be unpleasantly chilly.

At first Lorton refused to allow the absence of news to worry him. But it preyed on his mind, nevertheless. At nine o'clock on the Monday morning he drove over to Kiburn.

The Capri was parked outside. But Dougal didn't answer the bell. Lorton wondered if he'd chickened out at the last moment. He'd sounded nervous on the phone last night.

Lorton glanced over his shoulder and let himself into the flat with the key he had found on Celia's mantelpiece.

It was colder inside than in the open air. The atmosphere was stale with cigarette smoke. Lorton looked quickly in the living-room, the bedroom, the bathroom and the kitchen. The flat was empty. It would be difficult to hide a cat in it.

He examined each room in a more leisurely fashion. The table was loaded with files and books about the Stuarts. Splashes of candle grease defaced a black-and-white picture of a woman in old-fashioned clothes. The bedroom contained little but a bed, a trunk and an old photograph of Celia. The kitchen and bathroom were surprisingly clean.

As far as Lorton could tell, Dougal hadn't done a bunk. His cheque card was on the table. His passport and driving licence were in one of the box files. In any case, Dougal wasn't the type to run away: someone with his talents had nowhere to run to.

He used the telephone to ring his own number and Celia's, on the offchance that Dougal had gone to Primrose Hill. He rejected the temptation to call Celia at the office. She would only wonder why he wanted Dougal.

Lorton settled down to wait. He was good at that.

Georgina sank back in Ivor's chair. The foam rubber squeaked beneath her weight. She waved Celia to a seat and continued to browbeat Ivor's unfortunate secretary.

'It's *quite* simple, Fiona dear. Just give me a list of Ivor's appointments. In most cases there'll be no problem.'

'But Mr Newley said that Mr Brassard —'

'Well, Mr Newley isn't here today, is he? I'm quite capable of deputizing for my husband. I think you'll find Hugo will agree with me. Now, Fiona, I shall need you to brief me on some of the meetings, especially the visit to RTI. After we've discussed the appointments, I may need you to do a few letters.'

Fiona stared down at her bright red nails. 'Mr Newley told me to do the RTI expense sheet this morning.'

'If necessary it can keep till this afternoon.' Georgina's voice hardened. 'Close the door behind you, and tell Zaza I'd like some coffee.'

As the door closed behind the routed Fiona, Celia thought she glimpsed the worried, ageing woman behind Georgina's façade of gruff competence. It couldn't be easy to cope with the emotional strain of a missing husband and do his job at the same time.

'Any news of Ivor?' she asked gently.

Georgina ran a finger down the cutting edge of Ivor's paperknife. 'I've rung the police. They're sending someone round. I wanted to have a word with you about Yorick. Be candid. What was the concert like? Can we get any mileage out of it?'

The abrupt change of subject disconcerted Celia. 'It was awful. One of those situations when any publicity we get is bound to be bad.'

'I wish Ivor had been there. He might have been able to do something.'

'I doubt it.' Celia hesitated and then plunged on: 'I don't know if I should mention this, but Yorick was very upset that Ivor wasn't there. He took it as some sort of betrayal.'

'The absurd little man. I can't abide people with artistic temperaments: always blame someone else, never themselves. I just hope he has a little more success with *Mishima*.'

Celia nodded. 'So do I. To be honest, though, I don't think the album will make things much better. Even the concept's about fifteen years out of date.'

'We may have to cut our losses in that direction.' Georgina jabbed the point of the paperknife into the blotter and changed the subject again. 'How's the house-hunting going?'

It hadn't even started.

'Fine,' Celia said. She was suddenly tired of all the evasion, her own included; she had also had her fill of conversational shock tactics. 'In fact it's possible I may move in with William.'

Georgina raised her eyebrows. 'I'd think very carefully about that, if I were you. A woman needs her independence.'

Dougal was so cold that he dropped the key the first time he put it in the lock. The second time, his fingers hardly had the strength to turn it.

He stumbled into the hall, kicking the door closed behind him. The living-room door was open, and he could see that his duvet had migrated mysteriously from the bed to the armchair. He had barely registered this fact when he felt a tap on his shoulder.

Subconsciously he must have been expecting something like this: his first reaction was not surprise but an intensification of the dull misery which had enveloped him for the last 24 hours. Lorton came out of the bathroom. Dougal desperately wanted to run away; but Lorton was between him and the front door.

Lorton said: 'Why didn't you ring last night?'

His voice was not unpleasant. Dougal nevertheless remembered that the army had trained Lorton in the efficient use of violence; and that subsequently he had sold those skills to the highest bidder. *A merc fights for anyone, mate. Not Commies, of course. And never for anyone who means harm to the Queen.* It had struck Dougal at the time that Lorton's view of patriotism was more than old-fashioned: it was positively feudal, in that it depended on loyalty to a single person. He was terribly afraid that at present Lorton was loyal solely to his own interests. These thoughts were coloured by the depressing realization that a meeting between them was inevitable.

94

'Why don't we sit down?' Dougal said.

'Be my guest.'

Dougal sat in the armchair and wrapped himself in the duvet. It was still warm from Lorton's body. Dougal was too cold to be choosy about the source of any spare heat.

Lorton remained on his feet, his arms swinging slightly. 'So where's the money?'

'It wasn't there.' Dougal wondered how on earth he was going to play this.

'Really.' Lorton's tone meant *That's your story*. 'What about the guinea?'

'That had gone too.'

'You're saying that Newley worked a double-cross?' There was a faint, incredulous stress on the name.

'Not Newley.' Dougal stressed the name too. 'Newley was there, in the gazebo. He was dead.'

'Come off it.' Lorton's voice hardened. 'You'd better start talking. Fast.'

Dougal could have done without the B-movie dialogue. Crises thrived on clichés.

'Newley had been stabbed. His body was cold; I think he'd been there for hours.' He looked up at Lorton. *If he's the murderer, he won't kill me because he needs a scapegoat; and if he isn't, he won't kill me either because he's got no reason to.* It was time to move on to the offensive: 'What I'd like to know is how you managed to see Newley in Primrose Hill at six o'clock.'

Without warning, Lorton bent down and grabbed the edges of the duvet. He pulled Dougal to his feet. Dougal didn't struggle: even if he could have got out of the duvet, he wouldn't have stood a chance. Their faces were six inches apart.

'Don't monkey with me,' Lorton said. 'What have you done with the money?'

'It wasn't there,' Dougal repeated patiently. 'And if I had nicked it, do you really think I'd be here?'

Lorton released his grip. Dougal fell inelegantly into the chair. Lorton's face revealed nothing, but his voice had lost a little of its assurance.

'I didn't actually see Newley. Not then. Just his car.'

'Tell me what happened.'

'I saw him leaving Primrose Hill. He was alone, and in the BMW.'

'But you didn't see him come back?'

'I told you, I saw the car. It was parked a couple of streets away. I was walking around, keeping an eye out for him. The car wasn't there at twenty to six, but ten minutes later there it was. The engine was warm.'

The story was plausible, but that didn't mean it was true. It was supported by Lorton's apparent belief that Dougal had taken the money; but that could be no more than bluff. Lorton was staring fixedly at him. He was probably wondering if Dougal had killed Newley.

Lorton sat down opposite Dougal. 'We're going to have problems when they find the body,' he said casually. 'People must go up there even in winter. It may've been found already.'

'I hope not. You see, I put it in the pond. After last night's frost, the ice should hide it for a while.'

'That was stupid. You should've just buggered off.'

Dougal shook his head. 'You don't understand. I thought I'd been framed.'

'Who'd want to . . . ?' Lorton paused. 'I see. You thought I'd set you up, because I'd told you Newley was back in London. Thanks for the bloody vote of confidence.'

'Well, at the time it did look that way.' Dougal threw in the necessary lie: 'Of course, I realize I was wrong now.'

'Because I only saw the car?'

'That's one reason. But there was something else. When I moved the body, I found a cheque book of yours.'

'You *what*?'

'I've burnt it. The point is, I didn't think you'd be likely to make that sort of mistake. Which led on to the obvious conclusion.'

Lorton stared blankly at him. 'Which is?'

'That someone was trying to frame you.'

The smell of liver and bacon greeted Celia as soon as she opened her front door.

William was in the kitchen, stirring the casserole with one hand and holding a glass of red wine in the other. The oven door was open, and there were four jacket potatoes on the second shelf. The plates were warming under the grill. On the work surface she could see a bowl of salad, the wine bottle and a row of cutlery. *Don Giovanni* filtered through from the sitting-room. It was like coming home.

They kissed casually, as if yesterday hadn't existed.

'Dinner in about half an hour,' William said.

'I'll just get changed.'

The sitting-room was tidier than when she had left it. The ruins of the rack shelving were leaning against the wall; the books had been stacked up in neat piles beside it. The ashtray was empty, and it looked as if it had been washed.

While she was changing, William and the wine had moved in front of the gas fire. She sat beside him; he poured her a glass and put his arm around her. He still looked tired. They would have to talk about yesterday, but not yet.

'Good day at the office, dear?' he whispered in her ear, managing to lick the lobe as well.

Okay — we both want to keep the conversation in neutral.

She giggled, because he was tickling her. Then she pulled away. 'We had a real crisis today. Ivor's disappeared.'

William spilled a drop of wine. 'How do you mean?' He licked his finger and dabbed the mark on his trousers.

Celia told him the little she knew. 'Georgina's in quite a state, underneath the armour-plated shell. She was really nervous when the police came.'

'What did they say?'

'Apparently they weren't very helpful. About sixty thousand people vanish every year, and most of them turn up undamaged. It's not as if Ivor's a ten-year-old girl. And it looks as if Ivor was planning to do a bunk. Perhaps Arabella's death upset him more than he let on.'

'Why do you think that?'

'Georgina said she'd looked through his papers last night.'

'I'm surprised she doesn't do that as a matter of course.'

Celia ignored the interruption. 'She found he'd drawn out

97

quite a lot of money on Friday, from two building society accounts they've got. Ten thousand pounds. And he took it out in cash.'

'Celia?'

She murmured something he couldn't catch and flung her leg over his. It was after midnight. Dougal's body had flaked out hours earlier, but his mind wouldn't go to sleep.

'Will you come and live in sin with me?'

'Why?'

'Because Rod's selling this house. Because I'll have to sell my flat if you don't come and help with the bills. They cut off the electricity last week. Because it's silly to throw away money on two flats when one would do.' *And because I don't want you living in the same house as someone who might be a murderer.*

'Not good enough,' she said sleepily. 'Hugo would say you needed to sharpen up your selling-points.'

Dougal sighed. He had taken it for granted that the other reasons didn't need to be spelled out.

'I want you to. I love you.'

'Maybe I will. One day.' She buried her head in the pillow and began to snore gently.

Dougal even liked her snoring. He switched out the light and lay there, watching the little red numbers changing on the face of the clock. The arm which was trapped beneath Celia gradually went numb, like a partial foretaste of death.

Underneath the water, Ivor Newley's skin would have begun to bleach and wrinkle. Eventually, if the body lay undisturbed for long enough, the skin might even detach itself from the body. Dougal had read all about it this afternoon in the public library at Swiss Cottage.

There had been a case in Australia, back in 1933, when a body was found in a river near Wagga Wagga. The body had been unrecognizable, because decomposition was so far advanced. The skin from both hands had peeled away from the rest of the corpse. One of these glove-like objects was washed up on the bank. The police took fingerprints from it and identified the body. Later they caught the murderer.

98

Dougal slid into a waking dream. The skin from Newley's hands, semi-transparent without their former contents of flesh and bone, looked like a pair of pale kid gloves. They floated in front of his eyes, moving ceaselessly. He knew they were trying to tell him something in the sign language used by the deaf and dumb.

Over and over again, the hands danced through the same short sequence of signs. The name of the murderer? A curse? A prayer for mercy? A string of gibberish?

Chapter 10

'DOING A BIT of decorating, sir?' Detective Sergeant Maxham said. 'One way of keeping warm.'

'I'm putting the house on the market.' They could find that out easily enough, so why not tell them? Lorton wiped his hands on a rag. 'Do you want to sit down?'

'That's very kind of you.' Maxham removed an empty paint tin from the seat of the nearest armchair and sat down with a sigh of relief. 'I've got this verruca,' he confided. 'Gives me hell in the cold weather, for some reason. They say it went down to minus ten last night.'

Lorton perched on the step ladder. 'You should see a doctor.'

'What's the point? All they do is give you some ointment and tell you it'll drop out in its own good time. But it doesn't. Oh no. It's like trying to peel an onion. You spend twenty minutes on it every night, and you scratch off a layer of dead skin. But underneath it's just the same, except it hurts more. No, me and my verruca are together for life. Until death do us part.' Without warning, Maxham looked away from Lorton, towards the door. The good humour vanished from his plump, pink face. 'For God's sake, Bernie, park your arse somewhere. You look like a constipated panda.'

Detective Constable Viol chose a hard chair near the window. He was a bulky young man, who was wearing a black coat and a white shirt; the comparison with a panda was unkind but accurate.

Maxham was one of the chatty type, like a superior salesman, a foot through the door before you had time to register that someone was on the doorstep. Lorton had known who they were as soon as he'd seen them; he had been expecting the police, though not quite as soon as this, and in any case salesmen rarely travelled in pairs. Besides, Maxham wasn't dressed with a salesman's mass-produced smartness: he was a wiry little man whose rumpled suit and gold-rimmed glasses made him look like an old-fashioned country doctor.

Viol pulled out a notebook and a biro. He licked his lips.

'Bernie's such an eager beaver.' Maxham scratched a tweed-covered knee-cap. 'But I suppose he's right. You see, sir, we've got a problem. And I hoped you might be able to help us.'

Lorton said nothing. He had had dealings with the police in many countries. It never paid to volunteer information. There was nothing to worry about: if there had been, the fuzz would have come in with a warrant. They wouldn't be chatting about the weather and their verrucas.

'Missing persons,' Maxham said. 'Matter of routine. But in this case the routine's got buggered up, if you'll excuse my French, because someone's short-circuited the standard procedure.' He pulled a wry face, inviting Lorton's sympathy. 'Right now we've got a lady who went to school with the Assistant Commissioner's wife. You know how it is, Mr Lorton: strings are pulled, and we all have to go through the hoops rather faster than normal.'

'Is this about Ivor Newley?' Lorton said.

'You know about it?' Maxham began to scratch the other knee-cap. 'Let me see, it's Friday. Newley went off only five days ago. News travels fast.'

Lorton shrugged. 'My lodger works for NCPR.' He added, insultingly: 'Newley's firm.'

'Miss Celia Prentisse.' Maxham's pale grey eyes blinked. 'So she does. You used to work there too?'

'I resigned a few weeks ago.'

'Of course you did. I gather randy old Ivor was screwing your missus. Your late missus.'

One-all.

'We had a row,' Lorton said calmly. There were witnesses to that, so he might as well earn a bonus point by mentioning it first. 'Can you blame me?'

'If it'd been my missus, I'd've been relieved that someone else was taking an interest. Take the heat off me. Anyway, so you had a slanging match. You seen him since then?'

Lorton shook his head.

'Sure about that?'

'Yes.'

'The week before he disappeared, Newley raised ten grand in cash. What does that suggest to you?'

'You tell me.'

Two-one.

Maxham held up two fingers in an obscene gesture. He neutralized the obscenity by touching the tip of one finger. The V-sign became an inoffensive teaching aid.

Two-all.

'Either he was being blackmailed.' Maxham touched the tip of the other finger and smiled. 'Or he wanted to make a new start in life. Don't we all?'

'Maybe he just wanted to buy something.'

'Maybe. Just as a matter of interest, what were you doing on Sunday?'

'Nothing much. I went to mass in the morning.'

Lorton had woken up with the desire to take communion. Not because he was feeling religious. More to fill in time, and perhaps to find out if the God of his childhood really did exist, after all. He had half expected a divine pre-emptive strike, a thunderbolt maybe, as he queued for the body and blood. Nothing had happened. But he could still taste the sweet, rich wine —

'Catholic, are you? So's my old woman. Where did you go?'

'Saint Etheldreda's, in Holborn. The early service.'

It had been a stupid thing to do, on that day of all days. He might have missed Newley's departure. But he had needed to go. It was as if he was proposing a bargain to God: *I'll come to church, if You'll turn a blind eye later.* And God didn't even bother to listen —

'See anyone you knew there?'

'No. But I chatted with the priest on the way out.'

'Nice to see a new face among us. Shall we see you next Sunday?'

'I don't think so, Father. I . . . I'm just passing through.'

'Then I came home,' Lorton said. 'Celia came up to pay me the rent, mid-morning that'd be. I had my dinner. A bloke called Tolby came round — '

'Eustace Tolby? The solicitor?'

Lorton nodded. 'Around two o'clock, I think.'

'Any particular reason?'

They would ask Tolby that, if they hadn't done so already. But what would Tolby tell them?

'Search me,' Lorton said. 'Oh, he said he happened to be passing — you know, just popped in to see how I was, what a shame I'd left NCPR.'

'That surprised you?'

'A little. I saw him at work quite often, of course, but we were never exactly buddy-buddy.'

Maxham let the silence lengthen. The only sounds were Viol's heavy breathing and the scratching of the biro on his notebook. Then Maxham waved a square, clean hand, brushing aside Tolby for the time being.

'What did you do with the rest of the day?'

'I had a walk. Did a bit of painting. I went out for a drink just after seven — at the Sir Richard Steele on Haverstock Hill. Then I had a snack and watched telly.'

'You saw no one in the evening?'

'I think Celia was in. She probably heard the telly, and me moving around.'

Lorton had calculated the alibi carefully. If alibi was the right word. A completely watertight one was obviously impossible; and it would also be sufficiently unusual to be suspicious. In the circumstances it was best to leave himself room for manoeuvre. You could never tell who might have seen you. Or where.

Maxham took out something which looked like a piece of chewing gum. He peeled off the wrapper and popped it in his mouth.

'Indigestion,' he said. 'The copper's curse. That and alcoholism and broken marriages. It's the unsocial hours we have to work.' He chewed vigorously for a few seconds. 'Every job has its drawbacks. We never end up doing what we want. Bernie here, he wanted to be a deep-sea diver. I was going to be an engine-driver. *Real* engines, of course, not the diesel or electric rubbish they use nowadays.' Maxham sighed. His eyes lost their vagueness and focused on Lorton. 'And so we drift into something else. How did you end up in public relations, Mr Lorton? Bit unusual for someone with your background.'

So they knew about that. The old bitch would have told them. They would have dug out his file from the Ministry of Defence, and got chapter and verse on his time in the army. And that would have led them to their own Special Branch registry, where there must be a file on his career as a freelance; it was inevitable after that damned publicity.

Lorton shrugged. 'I was working for Custodemus.'

'The security people?'

'Yeah.' Lorton wondered what was the purpose of that unnecessary question. Perhaps Maxham already knew that the Newleys' burglar alarm was one of the early Custodemus models. But surely the police couldn't know about the burglary? Newley wouldn't have told Georgina. The only person who could have told them was William Dougal. But that was absurd.

'Everything from payrolls to personal security,' Maxham said. 'Plus a range of hardware to suit every pocket.' He made no attempt to hide the sneer. 'And what exactly did you do, Mr Lorton? Stroll around in a smart blue uniform?'

Two-three.

'I worked for personnel. Desk job. I did some PR, too.'

'And Newley made you an offer you couldn't refuse?'

'You could put it like that.'

'Darling,' Arabella had said, *'You know that PR firm I did some work for? I was talking with their boss the other day, and he said they were looking for new blood . . .'*

Maxham leered. 'Maybe Newley wanted to pay his way.'

Two-four. It was an unequal contest, and Lorton was tired of playing the loser.

He stood up. 'Look, mate, I'm busy. You got any more questions? *Real* questions?'

Three-four.

'Not for now.' Maxham took his time getting up. 'If we need you again, we'll know where to find you. You're not planning to leave in a hurry, are you?'

Lorton shook his head. Viol sprang to his feet, politely

drawing back to allow his superior to precede him. Maxham put his hand on the door.

'Mind the paint,' Lorton said. 'It's wet.'

Four-all.

From Primrose Hill, London looked like a ruined city, shrouded in mist.

The top of the hill was empty at this time of day. The weather kept away the housewives, the unemployed and the winos. In a couple of hours' time, the kids would be out of school and dogs would be out for their last daylight walks. The frozen snow would become a playground. The steep slope towards Regent's Park would be cluttered with death-defying sledges.

Dougal was wearing three jerseys and Celia's duffel coat, but as far as the wind was concerned he might as well have been naked. He wished Lorton had chosen a less exposed place to meet.

Lorton was coming up the path. As he came closer, Dougal saw that there was a drop of moisture on the pink tip of his nose. Lorton wasted no time in preliminaries.

'The police came today.'

Dougal had an instant of undiluted panic. 'Have they found . . . ?'

Lorton shook his head. 'It's just a missing-person case. Georgina's got friends in high places.'

'She would.' The panic receded for the time being. 'There's nothing we can do except sit tight, is there?'

'The longer they take to find Newley, the better it'll be for both of us.' Lorton paused. 'Though of course there's nothing to link us with him . . . disappearing.'

'Not now,' Dougal said. One of the unpleasant by-products of this affair was that it had blighted the beginnings of a friendship.

Lorton smiled without humour and changed the subject. 'I sold the half-angel.'

'*You* did?'

'Don't be stupid. I got a mate of mine to take it on Wednesday. He's got contacts in antiques — you know the sort of thing. Not exactly bent, more sort of unofficial. He came round last night with two-fifty.'

'It was worth far more than that.' Dougal shrugged. 'All right. You don't have to spell it out.'

'Less his commission of 20 per cent, that's a hundred each. Okay?'

'Okay.' It wasn't okay but Dougal wasn't in a position to argue. They couldn't afford the luxury of open-market values. He wondered how much Lorton's mate had creamed off on top of his percentage.

Lorton passed him a roll of ten-pound notes. Dougal didn't count them. At the back of his mind, he marvelled that Lorton had bothered to give him anything at all. *On the other hand, a hundred pounds is small change compared with ten thousand.*

'I'm worried about the rest of them,' Lorton said. 'I mean, it's not impossible that the police'll get a search warrant for my place. Unlikely but you never know. If they found the coins they might put two and two together. They know about the ten grand. Will you keep them for a while?'

They had agreed it was best to put the coins on the market one by one; a flood of rare coins, some without provenance and others with the sort of provenance which would interest the police, would be bound to arouse suspicion. It surprised Dougal that Lorton wanted him to look after the coins. It argued either that Lorton trusted him still, or that Lorton had in mind some devious idea of framing him. His mind went back to the familiar and unanswerable question: who killed Newley?

'Will you?' Lorton prompted.

Dougal nodded.

Lorton gave him a flat package, wrapped in a polythene bag. 'That's the coins and the letter to Tolby. I got rid of everything else.'

The drop on the end of his nose trembled and fell; it glistened like a snail track on his scarf. *Everything else.* Lorton's tone had given nothing away, but Dougal could imagine how he must feel. He might have destroyed Arabella's letters to Newley, but he couldn't rid his memory of their contents.

'How's it going then?' Lorton said awkwardly. 'You still involved with your Jacobites?'

'Nearly finished now.' Dougal shivered, partly because of the cold and partly because polite conversation was a bizarre activity for Lorton to choose.

Lorton moved down the path. He said something as he went, but the wind whipped away his words.

'Have you made up your mind yet? About moving?'

Celia shook her head. 'I don't want to make decisions at present. Don't rush me.'

William was sitting on the floor at her feet, leaning against her. She ran a finger down the nape of his neck.

He stirred and smiled up at her. 'I don't want to hurry you. Blame it on the electricity bill.'

'It's partly because leaving now would be running out on Rod. It's not just that he needs the money.' She paused. 'I can lend you some money, if you want.'

'No. I'll manage. It's only a matter of hanging on until the Jacobites are out of the way.'

She was immensely relieved that he had refused the offer. She didn't want to tie him to her with obligations. In the past she had been obliged to other people, William included, and it wasn't good for the character. It was easier to grant favours than to receive them.

There was another reason for relief. At the back of her mind was the half-formed worry that William was with her only for what he could get. She tried to dismiss the fear as the unwanted product of her own emotional insecurity. But it was impossible to forget entirely the rumours that William had been involved with some very undesirable people over the last few years. She had known William as a boy and as an adolescent; she was beginning to know him as an adult and as a lover; but between the two blocks of knowledge was a ten-year gap.

'When's Henry on?' William asked.

'Ten o'clock.' Celia welcomed the distraction. Henry's first appearance on television was due to a lucky prophecy he had made on the radio phone-in. He had predicted with uncanny accuracy the result of a snooker championship. NCPR was delighted, for television provided the ultimate publicity. Celia's stock at the agency had automatically and undeservedly soared. Henry had been invited on to the chat show chiefly because the new snooker champion was the guest of honour.

'I don't suppose his crystal ball's told him where Newley's got to?'

'He believes Newley's dead.' Celia cast around in her mind for a less depressing topic. 'What's happened to your coat? That grey one you got in the sale.'

'I lost it.'

She couldn't see William's face but something in his voice discouraged further questions. 'But how?'

'I left it in a pub. Someone must have nicked it. It was gone when I went back for it.'

Liar, Celia thought. Ever since they were children, Celia had been able to tell when William was lying. Not always, but a good 50 per cent of the time.

The ugly, unwanted question appeared in her mind: did she really want to live with someone who lied to her?

It was always worst at night, as he waited for sleep to rescue him.

Newley's body ambushed him in the darkness. Dougal's imagination presented him with images of decay. The images were more vivid tonight, perhaps because of the coldness which had developed between him and Celia. The evening had gone downhill since she asked about the coat. There had been no open quarrel — just the feeling that both of them had their heads down behind different barricades.

Celia lay beside him, breathing quietly and evenly. His hand was warm against her leg. He wondered if she was really asleep.

He tried to distance himself from the physical reality of death by thinking about the identity of the person who had caused it. The front-runner had to be Lorton: he had the motive; he knew where Newley would be; and he was presumably accustomed to the mechanics of killing. The cheque book, so conveniently left at the scene of the crime, could be interpreted as a genuine slip-up on his part. But Lorton wasn't a fool.

If it wasn't Lorton, who else could it have been? Newley might have told Tolby about the ransom demand. Suppose Tolby needed money, or had some other reason for killing Newley? The thought fizzled out for lack of evidence.

Maybe the murderer knew nothing about the ransom, and had followed Newley or met him by chance at the gazebo. There was nothing to prevent escaped lunatics and psychopathic tramps from spending their Sunday afternoons rambling through Hampshire; they had to spend them somewhere.

Could Georgina have killed him? She knew the geography of the place; she might easily have followed Newley down to Miller's End. The problem here was the lack of motive. She had come to terms with Newley's affair with Arabella; she believed that she had her husband precisely where she wanted him.

Other candidates presented themselves: Brassard must know Miller's End and he might have come to hate being bullied by Newley; Yorick blamed Newley for his own failings, and was hysterical enough to kill on impulse; Henry, having predicted Newley's death, had a vested interest in ensuring that the prediction was fulfilled; Zaza might have been seduced by Newley and then spurned —

It was useless: he had no evidence. Dougal closed his eyes and tried counting sheep. Instead he saw a pair of gloves, suspended in water and waving fleshless fingers at him.

Chapter 11

YORICK SCREAMED.

Georgina's door was closed, but nevertheless the sound was audible throughout the office. The typing stopped. Zaza dropped a cup of coffee. Hugo Brassard looked as if someone had given him a present.

Yorick screamed again — the high wail lasted for several seconds before it ended with a sharp report.

'Hysterics,' Brassard said, with the air of a specialist making a brilliant diagnosis in front of a first-year medical student. 'And Georgina's slapped him. It's the only way.'

Suddenly Georgina's — *Ivor's* — door opened. Yorick shambled backwards out of the room. Behind him Georgina advanced like a victorious army. She stared unwaveringly at Yorick. Yorick glanced back over his shoulder. The sight of Celia and Brassard seemed to give him courage.

He stood his ground. 'You can't do this to me,' he said shakily. 'I'll sue. I'll — '

'Why don't you sue?' Georgina roared. 'Just try it.'

'I'll talk to the press — '

'What'll you tell them? That you can't pay your bills?'

'But I will be able to pay you. Give me a month. Two months, maybe.'

'I'm giving you nothing, you pathetic little pederast. Because you'll never be able to pay anybody. You're a failure, d'you hear? You're all washed up. The concert was a disaster. The album reviews were worse. And now you have the gall to tell me you won't pay our monthly account.'

'Why should I?' Yorick spat on the carpet. 'You and your precious husband did nothing for me.'

'You'll regret that.' Georgina picked up her umbrella and resumed her advance. 'You filthy drug addict. You're a cretinous has-been. And everyone knows it, even your gormless boyfriend. I'm surprised he stuck to you for as long as he did.'

Brassard cleared his throat. 'I say, Georgina —'

Yorick turned. Celia had a brief glimpse of a pale, unshaven face, a mouth incongrously decorated with lipstick, and pleading, bloodshot eyes. Then he was running down the office, howling like a bereaved dog. The door slammed behind him.

Georgina slapped the palm of her hand with the umbrella, reminding Celia of a staff officer with his swagger-stick.

'That's the last we'll see of him, I hope,' she said. Zaza giggled. 'Be quiet, girl.'

'Yorick's left his bag,' Celia said. She pointed to the foot of Georgina's desk. It was a shabby army-surplus shoulder-bag which someone had painstakingly embroidered with purple stars.

Georgina wrinkled her nose, as if the dog had left behind an unmentionable souvenir of his visit. She pushed the tip of her umbrella through the strap and scooped the bag into her waste-paper basket.

'What are you all staring at?' she barked. 'There's work to be done.'

She closed her door. The main office gradually returned to a semblance of normality.

Celia said quietly: 'I don't know how long I can stick it here.'

Brassard twitched. 'We must be charitable,' he murmured. 'Yorick was really being most offensive. Did you know that Cyril's walked out on him again?'

'That's all the more reason for Georgina to make allowances for him.'

'Georgina doesn't make allowances for anyone.' Brassard lowered his voice still more. 'Actually, I wonder if it's — well, to be blunt — her time of life.'

'Her time of life?' Celia said loudly; she ignored Brassard's agonized expression. 'If you ask me, she's having the time of her life. That's what I object to.'

On Tuesday evening, Lorton bought a copy of the *Standard*. All he wanted was the estate agents' advertisements. But he never reached them.

The story was splashed over the front page, elbowing aside the arms talks and the council scandal. Lorton glanced through it and went home immediately. Celia's car was outside.

He called down the stairs to the basement. Her white face stared up at him. She looked tired but that was all.

'Have you seen the *Standard*?'

'No. I usually get one, but I had to go up to Hertford this afternoon. You'll get one at the station.'

'I've got one already.' Lorton clattered down the stairs. 'There's bad news I'm afraid — '

Her face went blank with panic. He could see her mouth forming a W. Dougal was a lucky bastard, and no mistake.

'It's Yorick,' he said quickly. There wasn't any way to do this tactfully. 'Suicide.'

Celia held out her hand for the paper. Rock Star's Harakiri.

Yorick had disembowelled himself, messily but effectively, with his samurai sword. He had chosen to do it before the statue of Eros at Piccadilly Circus.

Lorton put his hand under Celia's arm. 'I'll ring William. Is he over in Kilburn?'

'It was little better than murder,' Celia said fiercely. 'You do see that, don't you?'

Dougal resisted her efforts to pull her hand away from his. It was Wednesday morning. They had spent the previous evening and half the night talking round the same subject. He was beginning to feel that he had had enough of Yorick.

'They said on the news that Yorick was chockful of amphetamines,' he said patiently, for the third time. 'He probably thought everyone was persecuting him. He has to bear some responsibility for what happened.'

'It wouldn't have happened if that — that *cow* hadn't destroyed him in public. You weren't there, William. She ripped him into little pieces. It was totally unnecessary. *And* she enjoyed it.'

'I'm not defending Georgina —'

'Yes, you are.'

Celia was beautiful in a rage, Dougal thought. And he liked her like this, when she was rumpled with sleep and undefended by make-up. They were in bed, which was a suitable place for erotic thoughts; but now was hardly the right time.

'It's ten o'clock,' he said. 'Aren't you going into work today?'

She shook her head, violently.

'Do you want me to ring and say you're ill?'

Another shake.

Dougal repressed the temptation to sigh. He wanted a cigarette, but that would have to wait too. He put his arm around her, and after a while she began to cry. They were tears of anger, not weakness. It occurred to him for the first time that Celia would be a bad enemy, just as she was a good friend.

As for himself, he was sorry she was upset — and also, if he was honest, a little irritated too, because the crisis had wrecked his plans for the morning. But he found it difficult to feel much pity for Yorick.

Yorick had died as he had lived — untidily and selfishly. And that, Dougal told himself, was the cold, unpalatable truth. It was so unpalatable that he doubted if Celia's digestion was capable of handling it.

The crying wore itself out. Dougal passed her a tissue. She blew her nose and announced that she was going to have a bath. Then she would drive down to NCPR and resign.

'Leave it till tomorrow morning,' Dougal suggested. 'It's a big decision. Don't rush it.'

'I'm not going to change my mind.'

He dropped a kiss on her head. 'I know you're not. But if you're going to make a gesture, it's best not to do it while you're white-hot. It'll turn into melodrama if you're not careful. You'll upset Georgina much more, and yourself much less, if you do it in cold blood.'

Her body twisted in his arms. 'You're so calculating sometimes.' She looked up at him; her face was as hard as he had ever seen it. 'But perhaps you're right.'

*

When Celia reached the office on Thursday morning, Georgina wasn't there. The need to delay her resignation infuriated Celia. It was one more item to be added to the debit side of Georgina's account. She walked into Brassard's office and closed the door.

'Hullo,' he said. 'Feeling better?'

'Feeling . . . ? I wasn't ill, Hugo.' She steam-rollered over his surprise. 'Where's Georgina?'

'She's gone to the press conference at the record company.'

'Yorick's?'

Brassard's hand fluttered over his crowded in-tray. 'I was forgetting — you haven't heard. We were rushed off our feet yesterday. He was in all the dailies, and you probably saw the TV coverage. There's going to be a sort of memorial documentary at the weekend, on BBC1. The demand for *Mishima* has been quite incredible — '

'The ultimate PR coup,' Celia said harshly. 'Death.'

'Well, I wouldn't put it quite like that. But it's certainly — how can I put it — the silver lining. I'm sure Yorick would have wanted us — '

'Yorick doesn't want anything now.'

'Yes, of course.' Brassard avoided her eyes. 'Actually, it's more what Georgina wants.' He glanced slyly at her and then back to the filing cabinet three feet away from where she was standing. 'I didn't realize it until yesterday, but Georgina has a personal stake in Yorick's success. Or failure.'

'What do you mean?'

'She owns about 40 per cent of Mercutio Records.'

Celia sat down. 'So that's why she and Ivor took Yorick on.'

Brassard gave her a quick, intelligent nod. 'Yes. I'd wondered about that too.'

'The bloody vulture.'

'Perhaps that's a little strong. She's just a good business-woman.'

'When's she due back?'

'Any time. Certainly before twelve, because she's got a meeting here with someone from Gasset and Lode.'

Celia knew the name. Gasset and Lode was an American-owned paperback publisher which specialized in film and television tie-ins, soft pornography and celebrity biographies. *Celebrity biographies* —

'*The Journal of a Fallen Angel*?'

Brassard rummaged in his in-tray and pulled out a large brown envelope. He passed it to Celia.

'It's rather more commercial now,' he said. 'Especially if we can get it into the shops quickly.'

'She doesn't miss a trick, does she?' Celia weighed the envelope in her hand. Yorick would have been delighted to have it published. 'How did Georgina get it? Doesn't it belong to Yorick's estate?'

'Yorick left it here on Tuesday, just before . . .' Brassard cracked his knuckles in some embarrassment. 'You remember he left his bag behind? I thought I'd better rescue it before it went out with the rubbish.'

Hugo's nosiness had paid off again, Celia thought.

'As for the legal position,' he continued, 'I gather that Yorick died intestate. The next-of-kin is his mother. Eustace Tolby went down to see her yesterday, and got her to sign something. It's all above board.'

'But surely the police should have this?' Celia said. 'It must be evidence, if only about Yorick's state of mind.'

'The police have the original. That's a photocopy. Georgina had it done before she called them. The only problem is, as it stands it's almost unreadable.'

'It needs retyping?'

'That too. But I meant content rather than presentation. And there are a few rather unflattering references to NCPR. Georgina wants me to tidy up the manuscript before she lets Gasset and Lode have it. I don't suppose you'd care to have a look at it? I haven't a moment to call my own at present.'

Celia shook her head. 'I'm resigning, Hugo. As soon as Georgina gets back.'

Brassard stared at her with his mouth open for a full five seconds. 'But you can't do that. You know we're short-handed.'

'I can't help that. I don't approve of Georgina's methods. That's all there is to it.'

'Couldn't we come to some arrangement? Georgina has often said how highly she values your . . . If more money would help . . . ?'

Celia shook her head. She wanted to say that her conscience wasn't for sale; but she lacked the nerve. Having to take notice of your moral scruples was bad enough: parading them in front of other people was unbearable.

'No, it wouldn't help.' Brassard smiled unexpectedly at her. 'I'm sorry. Look, will you work out your month's notice? Henry will suffer if you don't, and so will RTI. If it comes to that, so would I.'

'I was going to in any case. It's in the contract. Besides, it'll give me time to look round for something else.'

'Perhaps I can help there. I've often thought myself — ' Brassard hovered on the brink of a confidence but pulled himself back just in time. 'About the *Journal* — do you think William might edit it for us? It's his line of country, isn't it?'

Celia's immediate reaction was to turn down the offer. But it occurred to her that she had no right to make the decision for William. She knew that he had nearly finished with the Jacobites; and as far as she was aware he had nothing else lined up. And he would certainly welcome the money. She hoped that he would refuse the commission, but her feelings were beside the point.

'What exactly would you want him to do?'

'Retype it — some of it's handwritten, I'm afraid. Cut out some of the obscurer passages, and anything too tactless. Just tidy it up, really. I'm sure we would pay a very reasonable fee for a rush job. Or perhaps an hourly rate — what do you think? The one consolation is that it's relatively short.'

Celia shrugged. 'I can ask him.'

'Would you?' Brassard's relief showed on his face. 'Why not take the manuscript home with you today? See what he thinks. I'd be so grateful.'

'All right. But I can't promise anything.'

Brassard's door opened without warning. Georgina stood on the threshold. Beneath her mink she wore a blue dress which made her look like an overgrown Girl Guide.

'*Wonderful* news! The *Mail on Sunday* is going to do a feature. We're going to use Arabella's photographs — so fortunate we had them done. And Mercutio have dug up some old videos for the documentary.'

'Splendid,' Brassard said.

'Celia, I want you to get in touch with Ronnie Thrale at London Weekend. Once ITV realize the BBC are going ahead —'

'Georgina,' Celia said. 'Will you be quiet for a moment?'

'I *beg* your pardon?'

'I'm handing in my notice. And during my last month here, I'm not having anything to do with your plans for Yorick.'

'She just crumpled,' Celia said to William. 'I don't think anyone's told her to shut up for years. Then she tried to talk me out of leaving — laid on the flattery with a trowel.'

'You really are leaving?'

'In four weeks' time.'

Dougal smiled. He marvelled that throwing away a perfectly good job could make her so happy.

'Then we'll both be poor,' he said. 'You'll have to move in with me.'

'Perhaps.' Celia turned on the oven and put the wine in the fridge. 'Or perhaps I'll get another job. Hugo's going to ask around.'

Dougal had seen the label on the bottle. 'We're celebrating?'

Celia blushed. 'I know you like white Burgundies. It's a Montagny. Why don't you have a look at the manuscript while I get dinner on?'

She shooed Dougal out of the kitchen. He wandered into the sitting-room and lit a cigarette. Celia had told him about the *Journal*, and he realized she would prefer him to turn it down. But he was inclined to accept the offer. The timing was perfect. Besides, it could be very profitable: PR firms set an inflated value on their own services, and they expected others to do the same.

He pulled the photocopied manuscript out of its envelope. For a moment he had second thoughts. The *Journal* showed all the symptoms of being an autobiographical disaster area.

There were perhaps 200 sheets of paper, ranging from foolscap, densely packed with single-spaced typing, to what looked like a paper bag covered with faint hieroglyphics, possibly in pencil. Yorick had included several newspaper cuttings ('POP STAR WEEPS IN DOCK') and an old school report ('Stephen must try to stop biting his friends'). *Stephen?*

The text was interspersed with doodles, most of which were variations on the same theme: a roly-poly man wearing a bowler hat and smoking a pipe. One of the few exceptions was a full-page abstract sketch in felt tip; it was labelled 'Cyril's Mind (Rear View)'.

Dougal flicked through the pages, dipping into the typed sections; the handwritten portions could wait. Yorick had eschewed such simple guidelines as dates and pagination. Establishing a sequence for the material would be the first problem. Dougal wondered if the absence of upper-case letters was a conscious literary gimmick; alternatively, it might suggest a simple failure to master the typewriter's shift-key.

Matters were complicated by Yorick's style: his consciousness did more than stream; it gushed. He had an aversion for proper names, employing instead a number of poetic circumlocutions. The 'silken midnight cowboy' was a clear reference to Cyril, but who on earth was the 'bug-eyed monster' or the 'dead-skinned harpic harpy'?

my white cowboy cried and silly-billy spilt a splash of blood across his bosom. i longed for my muse to appear and scatter the philistines with a wave of her magic wand, her third, all-seeing eye, but i made do with a scented geisha . . .

That might almost be an account of the office party, when Cyril had tried to sit on Celia's lap. In which case, *silly-billy*'s identity was obvious if unflattering. Dougal turned back, hoping to confirm the theory by finding a mention of the new year.

my picture muse walking with her hound amid skies like pink paper flowers. and the furry monster was there and the church bells rang

*unceasingly, my muse was red with righteous anger, o my love, and her
hound barked at the furry monster and her frankfurter but i did not let
them see me for worshipping in silence is the artist's choice, that is the
way for growth. inner suffering purifies, makes clean, a catharsis.
monks must know. the way of the cross and the way of the needle lead to
the same crossroads. at the crossroads by hampstead tube station i lay
down in my heart and wept . . .*

Dougal frowned. A bizarre interpretation occurred to him. If
it was right, it complicated everything. He would have to tell
Lorton, if no one else. But so much depended on the interpretation: if only Yorick had contented himself with unvarnished
English prose.

Despite the gas fire and the central heating, he was shivering.
He pulled himself together and began to read.

'William! Can't you hear me?' Celia shouted from the
kitchen. 'Can you open the wine?'

Chapter 12

'FRANKFURTER,' WILLIAM DOUGAL said. 'German sausage: sausage dog: dachshund: Goo-Goo.'

Lorton pulled the paint-scraper along the window-sill; the blade bit too deeply, and he gouged out a sliver of wood. 'Damn.' The sense of what Dougal had said suddenly hit him. His voice changed to a snarl: 'Then why the hell didn't he say so?'

'Because he was trying to write deathless purple prose.'

'Deathless crap.' Lorton felt as though he was drowning. He groped for a lifebelt. 'It doesn't mean anything. All that stuff about purple flowers — '

'Pink paper flowers,' Dougal said patiently. 'I was coming to those. The day after your dinner party was one of those really bright winter days. Might have been summer if it hadn't been so cold. It was a Sunday, wasn't it? I went for a walk in the afternoon. The sky was clear blue, except for some little pink clouds.'

Lorton threw the scraper on the floor. 'Come on. I made a pot of coffee.'

He led the way from the dining-room to the kitchen. It was another fine winter day, just like that Sunday nearly six weeks earlier: the day before Arabella died. The colours were so bright they hurt your eyes. His were smarting now, as if he wanted to cry.

They sat at the kitchen table with the manuscript between them. Even the table reminded him of Arabella: it was one of the expensive bargains which she enjoyed finding at country auctions. Lorton blew his nose and drank half a mug of coffee.

'This muse of his,' he said at last. 'Why should it be Arabella?'

Dougal pointed to the page in front of him. 'This bit at the party, about the muse not being there. Don't you remember how Yorick made a fuss because Arabella hadn't come? The third eye's probably the camera lens — "my *picture* muse", remember. The geisha must be Zaza.'

'But there're no dates,' Lorton pointed out. 'And you said yourself that the typescript's not in any particular order. So how do we know it's that Sunday? Or even that it's a Sunday at all?'

'"The church bells rang": that suggests a Sunday.' Dougal paused. 'And the muse had a hound. You haven't got a dog. But that weekend you were looking after someone's spaniel.'

'Pumphrey. From next door.'

Dougal nodded. 'On the night before, didn't Arabella say that she took him out to Primrose Hill in the morning? Georgina must have heard. You remember — it was just as the Newleys were leaving.'

'What are you saying, William?' Lorton said quietly.

'It's all rather vague.' Dougal rubbed a fingertip round the rim of his mug. 'I know Yorick's dead. And the *Journal*'s not exactly a reliable record of what happened to him — or even *when* it happened. But it does seem possible that Georgina purposely waylaid Arabella on the day before she died, and that the two of them had a row. And that neither of them told anyone else afterwards.'

Celia had a pen in her hand and a blank sheet of paper in front of her. But her eyelids kept closing.

The sunlight streamed through the row of windows above the fire-escape door, staining the carpet and the walls with oblong patches of gold. Zaza and Fiona were discussing their plans to visit Top Shop in their lunchbreak.

Brassard was on the phone: 'The thing is, Jim, the rotary feed is a revolutionary new concept.' He yawned. 'I promise you, this is going to change the face of vending machines. They've been testing the top-of-the-range model, the one with the voice-activated selector, on site . . . Yes, at Heathrow . . . Of course it's fully computerized . . . And the public's response has been *fantastic* . . .' He yawned again.

Celia yawned in sympathy. What with one thing and another she hadn't had much time for sleep last night. Sometimes she thought that she and William both had a need to make up for those lost ten years. *Or to make the most of what they had, while they could* . . . She pushed the second alternative away from her. She didn't want to think about it, any more than she wanted to think about William's missing coat or William's doubtful past.

'*There* you are, dear.'

Celia blinked. If her mind were a warship, the crew would be rushing to their battle stations. Affability was the last thing she had expected from Georgina this morning.

Georgina plumped herself into the visitor's chair. She fired an opening smile across Celia's desk. Celia resisted the temptation to duck.

'Now what did I want to ask you . . . ?' Georgina bent down and scraped a piece of mud from her sturdy brown shoe. 'I know. Hugo said you knew Brigadier Fowler-Troon.'

The sentence was somewhere between a question and a statement. It took Celia by surprise. Was this something to do with Ivor Newley? *There's a word for people like you*, Fowler-Troon had said. *Unethical*.

'He knew my father in the war. I've met him once or twice recently.'

'Splendid.' Georgina transferred her attention to the other shoe. 'I wonder if you'd let me have his address?'

What's the old devil up to now?

'It's Ivor's wretched coins, you see.' An avalanche of mud cascaded into the waste-paper basket. Georgina straightened up. 'The insurance is due for renewal at the beginning of March, and I haven't the foggiest idea what they're worth now. Ivor's always adding to them, the naughty boy. It's so . . . *awkward*, him being away. I was hoping the Brigadier would have a look at the collection and give me an estimate. I know he and Ivor are interested in the same period.'

'I've got his address somewhere,' Celia said. 'It's either in my bag or at home. Hang on a moment.'

She knew quite well that her address-book was here, in her shoulder-bag. But the pretence of searching for it gave her a moment to think. Ivor was going to be furious about this. On the other hand, she suspected that Fowler-Troon would be delighted to have a private view of Newley's collection. But what would happen if Fowler-Troon found the coins which Newley was not supposed to have — the Jacobite Guinea, for example? Georgina didn't know what she was letting herself — and Ivor — in for. For an instant she wondered if she should try to warn Georgina. She rejected the idea immediately: the Newleys deserved to reap as they had sowed.

'Here we are,' Celia said. 'I've got a couple of phone numbers for him too. I'll jot them down for you.'

But why did Georgina want Fowler-Troon? Surely an insurance company would need a professional valuation? Besides, Georgina must know that Fowler-Troon and Ivor were rivals; and that was the blandest possible construction you could put on their relationship.

'Thank you so much, dear,' Georgina said. 'You've been a great help.'

Lorton wanted to hit someone.

He wanted blood to spurt, bones to break and the sound of screaming. The violence seethed inside him, like milk bubbling in a saucepan, trying to boil over and escape the unendurable heat.

The last time this had happened was in Belfast, when they had cornered that PIRA bastard in the cellar. *Killed while resisting capture* — everyone had accepted the report, though they all knew what had really happened. Lorton shut his mind to that. He wasn't proud of the ability to go berserk because it meant loss of control. An uncontrolled soldier was usually a dead one as well, in a very short time. And if you weren't dead, you had to live with what you had done. You couldn't win.

'It won't help,' Dougal said gently. 'Arabella's dead. Nothing will bring her back.'

Lorton slowly unclasped his hands. The nails had dug deeply into the palms, leaving bloodless, crescent-shaped depressions behind. They were still sitting at the kitchen table. The sun was still shining outside. He could see a handful of snowdrops in the little back garden. Arabella must have planted them. It was so damned unfair that she would never see them.

'But I want to *know*,' Lorton said. 'Is there more?'

123

In a strange way, Lorton realized, he was a little afraid of William Dougal now. Not physically; this was more the sort of fear you had as a child — *of ghosties and ghoulies and long-legged beasties and things that go bump in the night.* Dougal could read meaning into the meaningless, like a priest finding omens in the steaming entrails of a sacrificed animal. It unnerved Lorton, as he had been unnerved as a boy to hear the priest say that bread and wine was changed through the magic of the mass into flesh and blood.

Dougal pushed a sheet of paper towards him. 'Read that. No, not the bit about the party. The paragraph below.'

just now cyril has his head in the toilet. the visual image is so important as a complement to the sounds. we need more pictures. i have a line and think why wait till tomorrow, we are wrapped in the present, like a seamless and infinite cloak; past and future are convenient illusions. time passes into eternity, so i ring (eternal symbol) mr and mrs monster to fix it up but no answer. i ring & i ring & have another line or three and then i think that all i want is peace that passeth understanding and the phone is a barbaric instrument of torture and do i really want more images for people to stick pins in me. i wish i could ask the muse, she would know. oooowwww. cyril says i am vain but what does he know . . .

Lorton raised his head. 'I can't take much more of this rubbish. So he tried to phone someone?'

'I think Yorick wrote that whole page when he got back from the party. As a general rule, he seems to start each session on a fresh bit of paper.' Dougal's voice rose with his excitement. 'And it fits: you'd expect Cyril to be puking his heart out when they got home. Meanwhile Yorick was snorting something, speed or coke I imagine, and getting more and more manic. He starts thinking about the photos. Specifically, he wants Arabella to take some more. So he phones the Newleys to try to arrange it.'

'All right,' Lorton said. 'I'll buy it.'

Dougal glanced sideways at him. 'Yorick called the Newleys several times during that evening — the Monday evening after the party. And he got no answer. *But he should have done.*'

*

'Whatever happens,' Brigadier Fowler-Troon said, 'You may be sure I shall do my duty.'

Celia said she was sure he would.

He had taken her to Daudet's again. His telephone call had come shortly before lunch, while Georgina was closeted again with the elegant young man from Gasset and Lode. She had been expecting him to call, though not quite so soon as this. His motive was curiosity, thinly disguised as concern for her wellbeing. Georgina had contacted him immediately after her talk with Celia. The request to value Newley's collection intrigued him.

'But where is Newley?' he asked. For such a small man, he had an incongruously deep and booming voice. 'I mean it's most mysterious. People don't just *vanish*, you know. Have they tried the hospitals? Perhaps he's lost his memory.'

'Mrs Newley thought of that. So did the police.' Celia could see a pudding trolley approaching. On the top shelf was a silver tureen brimming with strawberries. Strawberries in February: her mouth began to water with unashamed greed. Strawberries *and* cream; and damn what it would do to her waistline.

'I wonder if he's done a bunk,' Fowler-Troon said. 'It wouldn't surprise me. Always thought there was something shifty about that man. You can see it in the eyes.'

'Strawberries, please.' Celia watched the waiter spooning the glistening fruit into a bowl. 'Yes, with cream . . . perhaps a little more.'

Fowler-Troon waved the waiter away. 'But if he has done a bunk, you'd expect him to take his collection with him, wouldn't you? Or some of it, at least.'

'Perhaps he did. Perhaps that's why Georgina wants you to have a look at it.'

'Now that's a thought.' Fowler-Troon frowned. 'Rather devious of her. But it's true I've got a pretty good idea what should be there. Newley and I have been bidding for the same things for years.'

'When are you going to do it?'

'Next week — probably Tuesday. I can't leave it much later

because we're off to Australia on Friday. My eldest daughter's out there.'

He chatted about the trip while Celia finished her strawberries. He and his wife were going for two months. There were grandchildren to be met for the first time.

Over coffee, the conversation worked its way back to NCPR.

'You thought any more about leaving? Wrong sort of job for a girl like you.'

'I handed in my notice yesterday.'

'Jolly good.' Fowler-Troon's smile was distinctly smug. 'I thought you'd take my advice. I'm sure your father would have said the same.'

'One thing struck me as curious at the time,' Dougal said. 'The light.'

Lorton swallowed the rest of his pint. The alcohol had blunted the need for violence, but hadn't removed it. The light could wait. He picked up Dougal's empty glass and elbowed through the crowd at the bar. The lunchtime crush at the Washington was beginning to thin; but the serious drinkers always gathered round the bar for their last stand.

'The light,' Dougal said when he got back to their table. 'It's a bit like Sherlock Holmes's dog.'

'Come again?'

'The dog was curious because it didn't bark in the night, when it should have done. The light's curious because it wasn't switched on.'

'The light in the car park?'

Dougal nodded. 'Why didn't Arabella switch it on? It worked perfectly well — they tested that.'

'Oh, for Christ's sake.' Lorton rolled his eyes towards the ceiling. 'She was in a hurry to get those photos up to the office. She knew her way. Why should she bother?'

'Rod, I was in the yard one night with Celia. The buildings block out the street lighting. If none of the office lights is on, it's pitch black in there. There was snow and ice around, too. And Arabella knew she was pregnant — she would have

126

wanted to take care. Of course she would have tried the light.'

'This is another one of your damned theories.'

'I know. But suppose Arabella did try the light, and it didn't work. Perhaps someone had taken out the bulb. It's easily accessible — I checked. And afterwards they'd put the bulb back.'

Lorton closed his eyes to shut out the sight of Dougal. The implications of the theory became suddenly and horribly vivid. It was almost as clear as if he had been there.

Arabella drove through the archway, revving the engine far too high, as she always did in the lower gears. The headlights sliced into the darkness. The gate swung shut behind her. She cut the engine and the lights. The portfolio was under her arm. She tried the switch, but the light didn't work. Probably she swore. Perhaps she thought of turning on the car lights, but decided not to; it would waste time, and it wouldn't be much use because the car was angled away from the fire escape. So she climbed the fire escape, briskly for she had always been brisk about everything, even making love. On each floor there was a darker patch, marking the recessed doorway of the fire-escape door. As Arabella passed one of the doorways, a pair of hands shot out. A push. A series of thuds. A scream. And then silence.

'Yes,' Dougal said gently. 'It could have happened like that.'

Lorton opened his eyes. 'You think . . . Georgina . . . ?'

'If we can rely on the *Journal*. A big if. But she quarrelled with Arabella on the day before. She knew Arabella was bringing the photos round late that evening. Ivor Newley was having dinner with Tolby that night — you remember? Georgina was most upset at the time. Yorick tried to ring the Newleys but got no answer. So Georgina wasn't at home either.'

'But why? Georgina knew that Ivor was having an affair with Arabella. She knew about his other affairs. They didn't seem to worry her.'

'I think this one was different.' Dougal hesitated. 'Because of the baby.'

Oh yes, the baby makes it different. Lorton felt the bitterness sweep over him. The baby made it different for everyone. It reminded him of his own inadequacy; it made Arabella's betrayal all the worse; it had given Newley the courage to think of divorcing Georgina. And how had the baby affected the ageing and childless Georgina?

'If I'm right,' Dougal said, 'I don't think she meant to kill Arabella. The fall itself didn't kill her — it was hitting her head on the stanchion; Georgina couldn't have planned that.'

'*Great*,' Lorton said. 'That's a real consolation. She just wanted to cause a nice little miscarriage, did she? Because Ivor would come to his senses if there wasn't a little bastard Newley on the way? How old do you have to be before you can have the privilege of being murdered? Before you count as human? That's one thing my church *has* got right.'

'Listen, Rod, we don't know for sure. The *Journal*'s not evidence, not in the legal sense. A court would laugh at it.'

'I'm not laughing,' Lorton said. He could feel a muscle twitching under his eye. He forced himself to sit back in his chair, to swallow more beer. It was vital to retain control. The rage ebbed away, leaving a residue of bitterness. 'Is this just a game for you? Or do you really think Georgina did it?'

Dougal ignored the implicit accusation. 'I'm not sure. It all hinges on motive, on whether Georgina knew about the divorce, and that Arabella was pregnant. If we knew that, I think we'd be beyond reasonable doubt. But she's not going to tell us, is she? And no one else can.'

The words set up an echo in Lorton's mind: he remembered Sue's death, and the doctor saying, *She can't tell us what the problem was now, Mr Lorton. And no one else can.* But Lorton had known. In his memory, Sue and Arabella were beginning to lose their separate outlines. Their deaths connected them. He owed it to Sue to avenge Arabella. You never quite got away from guilt; the priests were right.

'I'm going to find out if Georgina knew.' Lorton's voice sounded alien to himself. 'I don't know how, but I will.'

'I did have one idea,' Dougal said. 'A bit far-fetched. It probably wouldn't work.'

The control snapped without warning. Dougal's arm was resting on the table. Lorton slammed his hand on it. Dougal cried out in surprise: he jerked away; his glass toppled off the table and shattered. An ironic cheer arose from the crowd round the bar. Lorton leant forward.

'It had better work,' he said softly. He tightened his grip on Dougal's arm and gave it a little shake. 'Do you understand me?'

Chapter 13

'The *I Ching*?' Henry Magus said. 'Oddly enough, that would have been my choice, too. Most people go for the stars or the Tarot. Between ourselves, I find them a little too deterministic for my taste. And psychically speaking, I can't help feeling they carry a little too much excess baggage. You know what I mean: people expect you to talk about dark strangers from over the water and golden fortunes coming their way. A lot of them would be much happier if I wore a headscarf and jangled gypsy bangles.'

Henry raised himself on tiptoe and pranced across the room. 'Cross me palm with silver, duckie,' he crooned. He lowered his heels to the floor. 'Whereas nowadays we all prefer credit cards.'

'I can manage used fivers,' Dougal said. 'Will they do?'

'I'll give you a reduction, as you're a friend of Celia's. Ten pounds all right?'

Dougal nodded. He wondered what the full fee was. He was glad that Henry hadn't waived the charge altogether; you wouldn't expect an electrician to rewire your house for free, just because you happened to be acquainted. He had already put himself out by agreeing to see Dougal at such short notice.

'I know what you really want is just a demonstration,' Henry said. 'But we shall have to do this properly. Try to get rid of those sceptical preconceptions of yours, just for the moment. And now I must make a few preparations. Sit quietly and let your mind relax.'

Relaxation was easier said than done. Dougal was chasing a forlorn hope; and he wasn't even sure that he was going by the best route. Beforehand, the pretence that he was interested in putting together a documentary series on psychic phenomena had seemed a good one. Henry was certainly intrigued by the project. It remained to be seen whether he would be willing to answer the one question for which Dougal needed an answer.

There was nothing to be gained from worrying, not at this juncture. Dougal tried to follow Henry's advice. He let his eyes roam round his surroundings.

Henry lived in a small mews flat, just off Fitzroy Square. The living-room was no more than fifteen feet square; but pale colours and a huge window made it seem larger. The impression of space was enhanced by the furniture: it was modern, plain and expensive; and there wasn't much of it.

The room was restful partly because it was anonymous. It contained no clues to Henry's professional interests and gave few hints about his private tastes. The one exception was the display cabinet mounted on the wall: it held two rows of Staffordshire figures; their garish colours contrasted vividly with the muted pastels in the rest of the room. Dougal was particularly taken with a flat-back figure of Dick Turpin, debonairly moustached and astride a prancing horse.

Henry's preparations for the consultation were as methodical as a dentist's. He removed his jacket, revealing a dashing red woollen waistcoat, rolled up his sleeves and left the room. Dougal could hear him scrubbing his hands in the bathroom. When he returned to the living-room he was carrying an oblong package wrapped in black silk, a spiral-bound shorthand pad and a cylindrical container made of brass. He placed them carefully on the table in the centre of the room. He arranged two upright chairs at the table, side by side and facing the window. His movements were solemn and precise. There was no trace of his previous light-heartedness.

'It was traditional in China for those in authority to face south when giving an audience. So we face north and the book faces south.' Henry's voice had become slightly pompous. He unfolded the silk and revealed a blue hardback volume. 'This is the *Book of Changes* itself. Some people like to burn incense and kowtow to the book. In my view that isn't necessary. We have our own ways of showing respect. Would you come and sit here?'

Dougal, relieved that he wasn't expected to grovel in front of a book, joined Henry at the table.

'At this stage I generally offer to give an outline of the principles behind the *I Ching*. I find it helps, if the client is unfamiliar with the oracle. People sometimes have very unrealistic expectations. The concepts behind it may seem alien, but there's no occult jiggery-pokery about them.'

'Please go ahead,' Dougal said. 'I don't want to ask a trick question. Just something quite straightforward.'

Henry wrinkled his snub nose. 'I'm afraid the answer is unlikely to be straightforward. You'll understand why when I've finished my little lecture. Chinese philosophers proposed, long before Christ, that everything was perpetually undergoing a process of change. Eventually they divided this process into sixty-four stages. In the *Book of Changes* each stage is represented by a hexagram — a six-line figure made up of whole and broken lines. To complicate life still further, each of these lines is either strong or weak which modifies considerably the meaning of the hexagram. Over the years, texts and commentaries have grown up around the hexagrams. They develop, often in complex, symbolic terms, the meaning of the hexagram. All clear so far?'

Dougal smiled. 'As mud, I'm afraid. I don't see where the oracle comes in.'

'I'm coming to that. Think of it this way. Any question you put to the *I Ching* refers to a particular process of change. For example, "What will happen if I shoot Auntie Flo?" refers to the process of change which binds together you and your Auntie Flo. The process is rooted in what has happened already, in the past; the *Book of Changes* allows you the luxury of seeing how the process will continue in a hypothetical future — in this case, if you shoot Auntie Flo.' Henry increased his resemblance to a chubby robin by putting his head on one side and glancing sideways at Dougal. 'I should warn you of two things. Relating a question to the text of a given hexagram is often a difficult and frustratingly obscure business; that's why you need someone like me. Secondly, the *I Ching* can be uncompromisingly moral. Almost certainly it wouldn't approve of you shooting Auntie Flo. It won't condone evil.'

A moment's silence stretched between them. It was all

nonsense, of course, Dougal thought; but the quality of Henry's belief was beyond dispute and curiously impressive. For an instant Dougal wondered wildly if Henry had guessed his real purpose. Perhaps Auntie Flo had not been chosen at random.

Dougal stirred in his chair. 'How do you link the question with a particular hexagram?'

Henry unscrewed the top of the brass cylinder and shook out a bundle of sticks on to the table. 'I use yarrow stalks to obtain the response. I won't explain the method unless you want me to —it'll only muddle you. While I'm manipulating them, I keep your question in mind.'

'So the link is sort of psychokinetic?'

'Perhaps.' Henry sounded uninterested. 'The main thing is, it works. Jung suggested that there might be an acausal connecting principle linking everything in the universe at any one point in time: he called it synchronicity. So the seemingly random patterns of the yarrow stalks provide a bridge between your question and the relevant hexagram. It's important to phrase the question correctly. Perhaps we should discuss that now. Have you something specific to ask, or do you just want a general overview of your life?'

'I suppose we could ask its opinion about the documentary. Could we do that?'

'Of course.' Henry uncapped a felt-tip pen and opened the shorthand pad. 'How shall we put it? "What is your judgement on William Dougal's plan for a TV documentary on the paranormal?" That should do it. We must both keep the question in mind all the time.'

As Dougal watched, Henry's stubby fingers moved among the yarrow stalks. First he returned one of them to the brass container. He divided the remainder into two piles. The fingers moved so fast that Dougal found it hard to follow what was happening. Each heap was sorted and subdivided. Henry placed some of the stalks between the fingers of his left hand. Finally, he made a calculation, the nature of which eluded Dougal, and scribbled a number on the pad.

He repeated this process five times. The performance lasted for several minutes. Despite himself, Dougal began to wonder if there might be something in it. The chance distribution of yarrow stalks was leading with uncomfortable inevitability towards a hexagram. And the hexagram itself was the key to a verbal answer. Dougal almost felt he was tampering with something he could neither understand nor control. He was briefly tempted to stop the session.

Superstitious rubbish.

After the sixth time, Henry replaced the yarrow stalks in their cylinder and consulted his notes. He drew a column of six lines, four of which were broken in the middle; he scrawled a cross in the middle of one of the broken lines.

'*Meng*,' he muttered. 'I thought so.'

'I beg your pardon?'

'It's the name of the hexagram.' Henry looked straight at Dougal; his expression wasn't friendly. 'You can translate it in various ways. Immaturity, youthful folly, obscurity.' He opened the book and turned its pages. 'The *I Ching* often uses this hexagram to reprove a foolish or dishonest questioner.' He read quickly through a section.

'What does it say?' Dougal asked.

Henry closed the book. 'It confirms an intuition I had. There's no documentary, is there? You're tangled up in something which will probably end in humiliation. You're in a mess, William, and you're trying to be devious with me. You want my help, not the *I Ching*'s.'

Embarrassment paralysed Dougal. He felt like a child caught out in a lie. A sense of his own arrogant stupidity blended with the shame: he had underrated Henry, and perhaps the *I Ching* as well. It was so damned unfair that Henry wasn't the complete charlatan he should have been. 'Youthful folly' struck unpleasantly close to home.

'Are you going to tell me?' Henry asked.

Dougal shrugged. He had wrecked his chances now. Frankness was the only option open to him, and he had no faith in it at all.

'What I really want to know,' he said slowly, 'is where I can find Devenish.'

*

Lorton ran Fred to earth in a pub near the station in Acton. The little Ulsterman was playing pool with a West Indian who was roughly twice his weight. He gave no sign that he had seen Lorton, but he probably had; Fred had eyes in the back of his head.

Lorton bought him a pint of Guinness and a whisky chaser. The game was nearly over, and as usual Fred was winning, despite his opponent's longer reach. Fred made up for his lack of inches by waging psychological warfare in the form of a relentless monologue. Today he was talking about his job. He was an environmental health officer by title and a rat-catcher by profession.

'It's as true as I'm standing here, as God's my witness, there were two dead rats in the babby's cradle, one on either side of her. They were already beginning to stink, this was summertime, you understand. And the mother says, "The babby likes to stroke the fur, they're like cuddly toys"; and I says, "Jesus, woman, you do realize there's enough poison in them rats to kill a bloody army?"'

The game finished. Fred's monologue also finished, in mid-sentence. He pocketed his winnings and wandered across the room towards Lorton. A squashed hand-rolled cigarette dangled from the corner of his mouth.

'You're a gentleman, Rod.' Fred picked up the Guinness and swallowed half of it. He sat down and relit his cigarette. He wore a greasy purple jacket which was several sizes too large for him. People generally gave him a wide berth because of the smell he carried with him.

Lorton knew Fred too well to try to hurry him. The little man had two attributes which made him valuable. He was a natural survivor and a natural entrepreneur. He could sell anything; and he wouldn't get caught. Lorton had met him first in Beirut where he ran a short-lived but lucrative business selling the same medical supplies to more than one purchaser. Fred talked about greyhound racing until Lorton bought the second round.

'You got something for me?' Fred asked.

Lorton passed a small brown envelope across the table. Fred opened it gingerly and peered inside.

'An old thruppenny bit?'

'This one's meant to be priceless,' Lorton said. 'It's Edward VIII.'

'It's a private sale?'

'Of course. I'm acting for a friend of a friend.'

Fred nodded. 'Priceless, you say? You putting a reserve on?'

'A grand. I won't take less. And that's giving it away.'

'It always is,' Fred said sadly.

'I need it done quickly. In a day or two at the most.'

'You're pushing it, aren't you? I'll have to up the commission.'

'Come off it, Fred. You charge enough as it is.'

Fred flicked the envelope back across the table.

Lorton sighed. 'Okay. How much?'

'Thirty per cent. After all, it's a private sale for a friend of a friend.'

'What's that got to do with it?'

'Your friend likes his privacy.' Fred winked. 'Nothing comes free.'

'Devenish?' Henry said. 'Bertie Devenish? Why?'

'I can't tell you.'

'The word's "won't", not "can't". Does Celia know about this?'

Dougal shook his head. 'And I don't want her to find out.'

Henry stood up and padded across the thick carpet to the window. 'How did you plan to get me to tell you?'

'By saying that the documentary needed to face up to the frauds, if only to distinguish them from sincere practitioners.'

Henry turned away. With the light behind him, his dumpy shape was emphasized. 'For all you know, Devenish is still in jail.'

'I traced the case,' Dougal said. 'He was given a twenty-five year sentence, eighteen years ago. With remission for good conduct he could be out now.'

'Why come to me?'

'You were upset by that case. Professionally, I mean. If Devenish was free, I think you'd want to keep an eye on what he was up to. And I wondered if you had a personal interest as well.'

Henry gave him a quick nod, as if acknowledging that Dougal was at liberty to use his intuition too. He moved across to the display cabinet and picked up Dick Turpin. He ran his finger along the line of the highwayman's arm.

'It has a tiny chip. Just here, on the cuff. You wouldn't believe the effect it has on the value.'

Dougal joined him by the cabinet. 'You can hardly see it.'

Henry returned the figure to its shelf. 'Bertie could be very charming,' he said carefully. 'He was also an extremely gifted medium. That was the real tragedy.'

'*Could* be very charming?'

'I've not seen him since he appeared in court.' Henry sidestepped the question. 'I need to know more.'

Dougal sensed that Henry's resistance had weakened. He knew instinctively that the success of what he said now would depend on how he said it. Henry's aftershave was overpowering at this range. He edged away.

'It's not my secret,' he said slowly. 'But I can tell you this. I think someone has done a great wrong. Eustace Tolby —'

'*Tolby?*'

Henry's voice was rough with anger. There was a chink in the armour of his benevolence, Dougal realized; and it was well worth trying to exploit it.

'I don't think Tolby's responsible, not for this.' Dougal watched Henry's face: he could have sworn he saw a flash of disappointment there. 'The point is, he may be able to prove or disprove it. But he's not going to want to. I need to find a way to persuade him.'

The words trailed away to silence. Henry turned his head and seemed absorbed by his Staffordshire figures. Dougal hardly dared to breathe. Details presented themselves to him with unusual clarity: the sprinkling of grey hairs among Henry's curls; an ambulance siren and a helicopter fighting for dominance outside; and the dryness at the back of his throat which announced that his addiction to tobacco was craving to be fed. He could hardly have set about this more cack-handedly, he thought: he was asking a respectable psychic to supply him with blackmail material. Lorton would have a fit if he knew.

Henry sighed. 'Bertie's dead. He hung himself in his cell three months after the trial.'

'I'm sorry.' Dougal tried to disguise his disappointment: to have come so far, only to find it was a blind alley.

'I think you're trying to be honest,' Henry said. 'You're telling the truth, and you want to do what's right.'

Dougal mumbled that he hoped he was. His voice lacked conviction.

'I can usually tell,' Henry said simply. 'In your case you probably think you're acting out of expediency. But there's more to it than that.'

This time Dougal said nothing. It seemed that he had undeservedly passed an examination which he hadn't even known he was taking.

'Clare Devenish lives in Woolwich,' Henry continued. 'If anyone can help you, she can.'

'His widow?'

'No. His sister.'

Chapter 14

CLARE DEVENISH DROPPED one lump of sugar in her tea. The china was so thin that Dougal could see the level of the tea swaying as she stirred it.

'I knew there was something wrong,' she said slowly. 'No, suspected. And even that is putting it too strongly. I didn't want to admit I was worried, even to myself. You must think I'm very stupid. Or very cowardly.'

Dougal shook his head. 'Sometimes ignoring a problem's the best way to deal with it. If not the only way.'

A lorry thundered down the Woolwich Road towards Greenwich, making conversation temporarily impossible. Miss Devenish, obviously used to these interruptions, offered Dougal another digestive biscuit. She was a thin, slender woman, somewhere in the further reaches of middle age. Everything about her — her face, her clothes and the room in which they were sitting — was pale, as if the colours had faded with frequent washing.

'I don't think so,' she said. 'Not this sort of problem. Because one's involved whether one likes it or not, just by caring for the person concerned.'

'When did you begin to feel something was wrong?'

Her mouth twitched. 'There was something wrong with Hubert right from the start. I was five years older than him. He always seemed to need protecting from someone or something. He never wanted to fit in, that was his trouble. Even as a toddler. Then our mother died, and I'm afraid Father wasn't very good with Hubert. He had very definite ideas about what a son of his should be like. He didn't mind about me: I was just a girl.'

There was no bitterness in her high, wavering voice. Her father's attitude had been accepted at the time and accepted ever since.

On the pavement outside, two teenagers were having a lovers' quarrel. Clare Devenish eavesdropped unselfconsciously. Dougal couldn't see a television in the room. Perhaps the bay window provided a wider range of entertainment.

Opposite the window was a curtained archway. The curtains failed to meet in the middle, revealing a section of the room beyond: a high, narrow bed flanked by a massive wardrobe in dark, stained oak; a large crucifix with an unusually lifelike Christ hanging on the wall.

Clare Devenish lived in these two rooms. According to Henry, she shared the kitchen and the bathroom with her three lodgers, all single women much the same age as herself. It was a household of spinsters.

Henry had phoned to arrange the meeting. He said that Dougal was a researcher who was investigating the Devenish case. Dougal was relieved that Miss Devenish agreed so readily to see him. But Henry was unsurprised: *You'll be doing her a favour. She likes talking about her brother. She hasn't many other pleasures.*

The teenagers were passionately reconciled; they moved away. Miss Devenish sighed.

'Hubert's . . . special gifts began to develop when he was about thirteen. He did automatic writing and moved ornaments — that sort of thing. My father just pretended it wasn't happening. But he couldn't go on pretending once the school asked him to leave. They said he was disturbing the other pupils. Father was furious. Poor man. He was *so* conventional.'

Dougal glanced at her face, wondering if he had imagined that note of amused satisfaction in her voice.

'Father wanted Hubert to come into the firm — you knew he was a solicitor? The original idea was that Hubert would join after university, but he had to give that up. Then Hubert was going to be an articled clerk, straight after school. But Hubert dug in his toes. By the time he was eighteen, he was earning quite a lot of money as a medium. He could afford to go his own way. And that's how Eustace came to join the firm. He was a substitute for Hubert. The son my father wanted.'

'Did your brother go on living at home?'

'Oh no. He left as soon as he could. There were terrible rows . . .' The lips twitched again. 'I don't think Father ever saw Hubert again until the trial. Even then, they didn't actually talk. Father had a heart attack. But I kept up with Hubert. That's how I met Henry. Such a sweet man. He was the only one of Hubert's friends I really got to like. Most of them were rather odd, you know, apart from Eustace; but of course he was different.'

Dougal put down his teacup. 'Why was Eustace different?'

'He's a cousin of ours. Didn't you know? I'd known him all my life. And Eustace didn't believe in the paranormal. He and Hubert used to argue about it for hours, but they were surprisingly good friends, for all that.'

Miss Devenish sipped her tea; Dougal noticed that her cup was cracked; the best cup was reserved for visitors.

She glanced out of the window at the empty pavement. 'Hubert was very hurt by Eustace's attitude at the trial.'

'He stopped being friendly?'

'Like so many people.' She looked reproachfully at him, as if he had been one of them. 'Of course Eustace was trying to establish himself as a solicitor at that time. You can see why he didn't want to acknowledge a family connection with someone who was convicted of murder. But it wasn't very kind.'

But it was very sensible, Dougal thought, if you were afraid of being implicated yourself. Tolby must have had some way of preventing Hubert from talking.

Miss Devenish chattered on, talking about Hubert as a toddler, in the dock, at a séance and in his teens. She jumped backwards and forwards in her narrative, creating considerable confusion in Dougal's mind. Once started, she was difficult to stop: she had the trick of pausing in the middle of sentences rather than at their end, which made polite interruptions next to impossible. After a few minutes her voice began to grate on Dougal's ears. He seemed to have been stuck in this shabby, overheated room for days. He could think of no way of escape, short of downright rudeness.

He learned nothing that would be of much use to Lorton. It was true that Miss Devenish let slip a good deal of fragmentary information about Tolby. The picture that emerged was unflattering; but it wasn't much use to an aspiring blackmailer. It was no crime to be ambitious and greedy. Tolby seemed to have buttered up all the Devenishes for what he could get: the father took him into the firm and launched him on his career; Clare darned his socks and cooked him meals; and Hubert — if Henry was right — had put some business his way. But Clare seemed to know nothing of this side of the relationship between her brother and her cousin. When the Devenishes had nothing left to give him, Tolby abandoned them.

'Well, what would you do?' Miss Devenish said.

For once she obviously required an answer. Dougal had not been listening to her for at least a minute. He took refuge in honesty.

'I'm sorry. I lost the thread of what you were saying.'

'I was asking what you'd do if you discovered someone you cared for was doing wrong. There's no easy answer, is there? You can't just stop loving them because you don't approve of them. But you can't condone what they're doing, either.'

Dougal muttered that he supposed each situation should be judged on its own merits. He felt uncomfortable for another reason now: he suspected that, once her moral hackles were up, Miss Devenish would be implacable, despite her mild exterior.

She leant closer to him. 'I knew Hubert was up to something. He started buying expensive clothes, a car; he moved to a better flat . . . I could tell he was pleased with himself but a bit scared, just like when he used to keep the half-crown Father gave him on Sundays, rather than put it on the collection plate. And then I found out about his old ladies. I had to do *something*. So I went to see the latest one, Mrs Houston she was called. And I warned her. But that just made it worse. Because she had a row with Hubert and he killed her. It was all my fault, in a way. He held a cushion over her face and pressed . . . and pressed . . .'

Clare Devenish covered her face with long white hands and began to cry.

'All you've done,' Lorton said angrily, 'is make a lot of people wonder why you're so interested in Tolby. Apart from that you've achieved sod all.'

Dougal sighed. 'I told you it was a long shot.'

'It's not good enough.' Lorton lowered his voice. 'I hope you've got another idea.'

They were in the dining-room, and Celia was directly below in the basement's kitchen. Lorton could hear the clatter of saucepans as she prepared dinner. She had invited him to share the meal. It was six weeks to the day since the Saturday of Arabella's last dinner party.

'We've made some progress,' Dougal pointed out. 'We've confirmed that Tolby was almost certainly mixed up with Devenish. He'll be vulnerable there. We've got a few more names and facts to throw at him.'

'He's a lawyer, William. He's not going to be frightened unless we've got something he can't argue away.'

Dougal wandered over to the uncurtained window. He touched the fresh paint on the frame and made a face when he discovered it was still tacky.

'Well?' Lorton said.

'There's one way to frighten him.' Dougal swung round. 'And we both know what that is. But I don't want anything to do with it.'

Lorton opened his mouth to speak but something in Dougal's face strangled the first syllable. He looked round. Celia was standing in the doorway. There was no telling how much she had overheard.

'Dinner's ready.' She looked at Dougal. 'You were going to lay the table.'

'Up to eight litters a year,' Fred said. 'And the average size is eight to twelve. The females can start reproducing when they're six weeks old.' He propped himself on the pool table. 'If they all lived, guess how many rats there'd be in this country in five years. Give up? Twenty-five million. It's a fact.'

This time Fred was playing a small soberly-dressed man who looked like a civil servant. As usual his tactics were paying off. Fred had once told Lorton that he reckoned to make his beer money from playing pool, and perhaps a little bit over for the dogs. He never played in the same pub twice in the same month; even so, word got around among the regulars. But he rarely had to spend a lunchtime without a game.

'Now take Warfarin,' Fred advised his opponent. 'You need to eat maybe a third of your body weight before it kills you. Some rats are immune to it now . . .'

Today the rendezvous was in Hammersmith. Fred had worked fast: he had sold the thruppenny piece in under 48 hours, and during the weekend. Lorton waited as patiently as he could.

Fred slid on to the seat beside him. He raised his glass to Lorton.

'Twelve hundred. Not bad, eh?'

Lorton shrugged. He knew someone had a bargain. He edged away: at this range Fred's smell was overpowering.

'I took out my three-sixty,' Fred continued. 'And the keys, they came a bit pricey, I'm afraid. Had to go up to a hundred. It's for this year's model, you see. They've got a better lock. I had to get three keys: one of them should fit. Mind you, it could have been cheaper if you hadn't been in such a hurry. Maybe fifty quid, or even less.'

'It doesn't matter,' Lorton said. He pocketed the envelope which Fred gave him. There was no point in counting the money. There would be exactly £740, in used notes. Fred cheated his clients, of course; but he never did it at this stage of a transaction. It would be bad for business.

'Anything else I can do for you?'

Lorton shook his head.

'Always a pleasure to do business with a real gent.' Fred stared hopefully at his empty glass. 'Don't look now, but there's a man by the bar who keeps looking at you. Came in just after you did. Mate of yours?'

Over their table was a mirror, advertising a long defunct brand of pale ale. Lorton glanced up. He saw the rear view of a fat young man in jeans and a leather jacket. There was a mirror behind the bar too; the man was staring into it. His eyes, doubly reflected, met Lorton's.

It was Detective Constable Bernie Viol.

Lorton left the pub just as Viol bought himself a second pint.

He strolled up to Hammersmith Broadway. Viol abandoned his drink and padded after him, twenty yards behind. When Lorton stopped, so did Viol. The policeman made no attempt to conceal himself. He looked miserable, as if his jeans were too tight for comfort and his jacket too thin for warmth.

The Broadway was thick with traffic. Lorton hailed a taxi. Viol tried to flag down another, but the driver ignored him. He stood on the pavement, his arms folded across his belly, watching Lorton drive away.

It had been easy to get rid of Viol, Lorton thought: too easy?

A few minutes later, he paid off the taxi and caught a bus to Shepherd's Bush. The encounter worried him. Did Maxham know about the other meetings with Fred? Lorton hoped not. Viol had made himself obvious today; and presumably he would have done the same on other occasions. Fred was convinced he had never seen the man before. That was reassuring in itself — the Irishman had a highly sensitive nose for coppers; he wouldn't have touched the coins if he had caught a whiff of police involvement.

The simplest explanation was that Maxham was getting nowhere with the Newley case; and he'd sent Viol along on the offchance, to put a little pressure on Lorton and see what happened. Maybe the Assistant Commissioner's wife was breathing down Maxham's neck.

The bus dropped him off just before the Green. Lorton walked down the Goldhawk Road until he found a big hardware store. He wanted to buy a knife.

Given a choice, he much preferred knives to guns. They were direct and simple. They were difficult to trace and silent to use.

Celia spent Monday lunchtime with Henry Magus.

They met at his flat. He had prepared a pasta salad which he served with wholemeal bread and fruit juice. While they ate, the conversation was confined to business.

Tomorrow's Woman was mildly enthusiastic about a proposed series of astrological interviews with celebrities from all walks of life. The idea had been Celia's. The celebrities would be interviewed in their homes. Henry would cast their horoscopes, probing their pasts, presents and futures; as a bonus, the series would reveal the secrets of their homes.

There was even a possible link-up with RTI: the firm was considering an addition to their leisure software list, called Astrogaze, with Henry as technical consultant. Henry had agreed to use Astrogaze to examine the lives of his celebrities.

They took their coffee into the sitting-room. Celia admired the Staffordshire figures while Henry poured.

'Have you found another job yet?' he asked.

'I wish I had. Hugo Brassard keeps telling me not to give up hope.'

'But you are leaving?'

Celia nodded. 'That's the one thing I am sure about.'

'My contract with NCPR ends in April.' Henry fiddled with the handle of the milk jug. 'I don't think I shall renew it.'

'You've had enough of PR?'

'No, it's not that.' Henry wrinkled his nose. 'It's just that I don't think Hugo or Georgina would do the job as well as you do. Have you thought of starting up on your own?'

The question took Celia by surprise. Henry's loyalty touched her.

'It had never occurred to me. And I don't know if it's possible: I'm not sure I've got enough contacts.'

'Would you need capital?'

'It would help, of course. But I could always work from home. Contacts are the really essential thing.'

'Well, think about it, dear. I think you'd do very well. And you'd have at least one client.'

The idea caught Celia's imagination. 'Perhaps if I found a partner . . .' She grinned. 'It's absurd. Castles in the sky.'

'It's always a good idea to have a few castles up there. I'd still be a lowly civil servant if I hadn't had my castle.' He passed her cup. 'I never did a reading for you, did I? Do you remember? I was going to, just before Arabella died. Perhaps this is the right moment.'

Celia shivered. She remembered that party all too well.

'I don't know if I really want one,' she said. 'Would you mind?'

'Does it seem a bit sacrilegious to you?'

'In a way. It's illogical, because I'm agnostic about everything like that, religion included. But I don't think I want to know what's going to happen to me. And you might not want to tell me, if it's bad. I keep thinking of Ivor.'

Henry sniffed. It was clear that Newley's jocularity on that occasion still rankled.

Celia said, before she could put a brake on her tongue: 'You really think Ivor's dead?'

'I don't think,' Henry said impressively. 'I know. And I know more than that. He died by asphyxiation, somewhere in London. It wasn't an accident, and he didn't do it himself. He was murdered.'

For a moment Celia almost believed him.

Chapter 15

TOLBY FLICKERED IN and out of sight as he walked along the
line of parked cars.

Sometimes you could see only his head or his legs; sometimes
you could see nothing at all. He was walking quickly with his
head down, running on invisible rails.

Lorton pulled back so that the concrete pillar concealed him
completely. The atmosphere stank of exhaust fumes. The multi-
storey car park was full of slamming doors and revving engines.

Suddenly he despised Tolby, with a venom which took him by
surprise. The solicitor had walked from the station to the car
park so many times that he no longer noticed his surroundings.
He was defenceless. The disdain spilled over and spread to the
other commuters scurrying to their cars. Did they never rebel
against the awesome formality of their lives? They had reduced
existence to the two secure havens of home and office. The
journey between them was as familiar to them as sleep. They
were only half alive.

His mind concentrated itself on Tolby's footsteps which were
slightly uneven, as if the solicitor had a slight limp. Lorton was
breathing quickly through his mouth.

Tolby unlocked the driver's door of the blue Volvo. He flung
his briefcase and umbrella on to the back seat. The car vibrated
as he climbed in.

Lorton slid from the shelter of the pillar, opened the passenger
door and got in. The car smelled of fresh plastic. He closed the
door behind him and smiled at Tolby.

Tolby's reactions were sluggish; Lorton could read them on
his face, seconds after the event which produced them. First
came surprise, swiftly followed by outrage; then recognition and
a corresponding relief; finally there was curiosity, leading to
confusion.

'Rod . . . You gave me quite a shock.' Tolby smoothed back the tufts of hair above his ears and tried to smile back. 'How did you get in? I'm sure I locked that door.'

Lorton held up the key which Fred had got for him. The knife was still out of sight, in the palm of his other hand. He said nothing and waited for Tolby to grasp the implications.

Tolby frowned. 'What is all this?' His voice was tetchy, but not alarmed. Physical fear was somewhere in his emotional vocabulary but over the years he had mislaid its meaning. Fear was something felt by other people when they found an unexpected lump under their arm or were mugged by a complete stranger.

Lorton uncurled his fingers, allowing Tolby to see the knife. It was a clasp knife, the sort that fishermen used for gutting fish. He opened it with a click, holding it in his left hand. The four-inch blade locked in place. Tolby was having a little difficulty with his breathing. Lorton stabbed him in the thigh.

He did it carefully. The tip slid through the tweed and penetrated about a quarter of an inch into the fleshy part of the leg.

Tolby squealed and jerked away. He tried to grab the knife. Lorton twisted it in the wound. With his other hand, he caught Tolby by the neck and pushed upwards against the chin. The back of Tolby's head collided with the window of the driver's door. His hands clutched Lorton's arm, trying to ease the pressure on his windpipe.

'Now listen.' Lorton shifted his grip on the throat. 'Just do as I say and you'll be all right.' He gave the knife another twist. 'You can let go of me, for a start.'

Tolby's hands fell away from Lorton's arm.

Lorton slackened his grip. 'Start the engine. I'll tell you where to go. If you make any mistakes, I'll turn you into a eunuch.'

The engine fired at the second attempt. Tolby edged the car into the queue. He sat well forward on his seat, with his hands clamped round the steering wheel. Lorton was relieved that the clutch gave him no trouble: the wound in his leg had been designed to scare him, not to incapacitate him.

Lorton realized that, when they reached the exit, the attendant might be able to see into the car. He switched the knife to his right hand, pulled back Tolby's coat and jacket and rested it on the waistband of his trousers. Tolby tensed himself.

The knife point pricked the skin.

The received military wisdom on prisoners was that time was on the captor's side. The longer you held someone, the more his will conformed to yours.

It was easier once they were moving. The heavy traffic gave Tolby plenty to do. They turned right out of the approach road to the car park, drove past Richmond Station and turned left on to the A316. By now the evening rush hour was past its peak. The Volvo picked up speed.

'I don't believe this,' Tolby said. He waited a few seconds for Lorton to reply. 'Jenny will wonder where I am. We've got people coming to dinner.'

They were slowing for a roundabout.

'Straight on,' Lorton said.

'Be reasonable, Rod. If there's a problem, I'm sure we can sort it out.'

Lorton probed with the knife. The car veered into the outside lane.

'Eyes on the road, Eustace. You're good at solving problems. You used to solve them for Hubert Devenish, didn't you?'

'I don't know what you mean.'

'Keep within the speed limit.' Lorton paused for a few seconds. 'I've talked to Clare Devenish. She found a diary of her brother's. She's prepared to testify.'

The Volvo bucked as Tolby braked without warning.

'Don't do that again,' Lorton said, 'or my hand might slip. If she talked, the Law Society could be very interested in you. But she might not talk. Did I say that she's given me the diary?'

He used the knife to distract Tolby's attention. The mention of Devenish should unsettle the man, but it was vital to prevent him from thinking too hard. The Devenish story was full of holes. Before Tolby had stopped squirming, Lorton flung another question at him.

'When did Georgina find out that Ivor was playing around with my wife?'

'How should I know?'

Another roundabout appeared. This time they had to stop. Tolby flung himself sideways, his hand groping for the door handle. Lorton grabbed his collar and pulled him back. He banged Tolby's head against the steering wheel. A car hooted behind them. Lorton wondered how much the driver had seen.

'Drive on.'

Tolby obeyed. Blood dribbled from his nostrils. In this light it looked black.

'I can kill you, or disgrace you,' Lorton continued. 'And either way I'll make you suffer first. Don't mess me around, all right? When did she find out?'

The silence lasted a few seconds.

'The week before Arabella died.' Tolby sniffed twice. 'Friday, perhaps, or Saturday.'

Lorton relaxed. 'How?'

'I'm not sure. Ivor thought she might have gone through his briefcase and found a letter from me. He told me about it when I had dinner with him on the Monday evening. He'd had a row with Georgina on the Saturday.'

'The row was about his plans for divorce?'

Tolby nodded. 'He was determined to go ahead. But then Arabella died, and there was no point.'

'Georgina knew about the baby too?'

'Ivor said that was the worst thing about it.' Tolby glanced at Lorton. 'Babies aren't her favourite subject at the best of times. She wasn't able to have any herself.'

'What stopped her?'

'One of these inherited conditions. Something to do with the hormones? I never knew the details.'

Lorton told Tolby to take the next left turn. Until they reached the outskirts of Teddington they drove in silence, except for Lorton's directions and Tolby's sniffs.

'Where's Ivor gone, Eustace? He must have told you.'

Tolby shrugged. 'He didn't confide in me.'

The solicitor's face gave nothing away. But he had called on

Lorton on the Sunday of Newley's disappearance. Newley must have put him up to it. Did that mean that Tolby had some inkling about the theft of the coins and Newley's suspicions about the identity of the thief?

'You must have an idea,' Lorton said.

'If you ask me, he ran away from Georgina.' Tolby snorted. 'I'd have done it years ago.'

'I thought they'd patched things up?'

'Only temporarily. Perhaps Ivor found the price he had to pay was too high. He's not a man who takes kindly to being henpecked. I know he was thinking about divorce again, but Georgina wouldn't have made it easy. I reckon he just took the easy way out.'

It sounded plausible, but the words were a little too pat for Lorton's liking. The solution was so convenient — and for someone in Tolby's position so tactful too. Tolby might suspect that Lorton had a hand in Newley's disappearance, despite the fact that he had unwittingly provided Lorton with a partial alibi for that Sunday.

But there was another possibility. Maybe Tolby had a different problem on his mind.

'Pull over and park,' Lorton said. 'Not on a yellow line.'

Tolby drew up outside a newsagent's. 'You mean . . . we've finished?'

'Not quite. Why was Newley having a second go at divorce?'

Tolby's hands trembled on the wheel. 'I told you. Georgina —'

Lorton ran the knife along Tolby's trouser leg. The blade sliced into the thick material. Tolby flinched as it touched the skin.

'I want the real reason.'

'You mustn't take this too seriously.' Tolby swallowed. 'I'm sure he was wrong. He was so upset about Arabella, you see, he wasn't thinking straight. He started wondering if Georgina could have killed her. Her and the baby.'

Celia spent another evening without William. It was particularly annoying because she wanted to tell him about Henry's suggestion.

It was one of those grey February evenings when winter seemed a permanent fixture. She forced herself to go to the cinema knowing that otherwise she would grow increasingly depressed at home.

The money was wasted because she couldn't concentrate on the film. Her mind was determined to dwell gloomily on the future. She needed to come to a decision quickly. In a few weeks she would part company with NCPR. Her savings should tide her over two or three months at her present rate of expenditure. If she economized, and perhaps moved in with William, she could probably last for longer. But unemployment didn't appeal to her. It wasn't just the money: self-esteem came into it as well.

The alternative was to use her capital to set herself up in business. An office was at present out of the question; she would need to work from home, relying on the phone. How would potential clients respond to a PR consultant who lacked an office?

If you came to that, how would William react to having someone else working in his living-room? It wasn't as if you could rely on him being away from home during the working day.

That was another depressing thing about this evening. Wherever a train of thought started, all lines led to the terminus of William. But William wasn't there.

William Dougal was drinking his third orange juice of the evening.

He had declared this week an alcohol-free zone after a bad hangover on Sunday morning. He had anticipated that going to a pub would test the resolve to its limits. So far the results were not encouraging. The resolve had held, but the orange juice was giving him stomach ache.

Lorton, by contrast, was drinking lager and thriving on it.

'No, Tolby won't talk.' He smiled reminiscently. 'I scared him shitless. Most people are soft, you know. They can't handle violence. It's a mental thing. They just go to pieces.'

His eyes met Dougal's; Dougal looked away. The words were a warning. He was going to pieces inside, just as Lorton intended, and he didn't like it. Being bullied make him angry.

'What about Clare Devenish?' he said.

'He won't go near her. I warned him off. Besides, I said I had Bertie's diary now, so it wouldn't do him no good.'

'I hope you're right.'

'I nearly forgot,' Lorton said. 'I've got three hundred and seventy quid for you.'

He passed the roll of notes beneath the table. Dougal stuffed them into his pocket. The money was the one bright spot the evening had produced so far, the carrot to the threat of the stick. Lorton's techniques were crude, but unfortunately they were also effective. Dougal decided that he preferred Lorton when he wasn't being cheerful.

They were sitting in a pub in Kingly Street. Their table was in the corner by the juke box; pop songs from the 1960s made an aural barrier between them and the rest of the clientele.

Dougal wished he was with Celia in her flat, watching something mindless on television. She seemed to believe him when he invented another meeting with Verrall, to discuss the Jacobite research. But lying to Celia was making him increasingly uncomfortable. Not only was she bound to find out sooner or later, but he didn't want to lie to her. Once he was out of this mess, they could start afresh. He would be truthful, decent and honest, like the advertisements.

'We've cracked it,' Lorton said. 'Tolby said that Newley tried to ring Georgina on the Monday evening. She didn't answer, just like when Yorick tried. She told Newley she was on the loo. But she can't have spent all evening on the loo, can she?'

'It depends,' Dougal said. 'She might have had —'

Lorton brushed aside the interruption. 'And it looks as if Ivor had come to the same conclusion. It's the only real explanation Tolby had for him starting up the divorce proceedings again. And it makes sense: Ivor's been married to her for years — he'd need a good, strong reason to go.'

'But it's not proof,' Dougal said. At this moment he would have argued with anything Lorton said.

'Well, what more do you want? Georgina's vicious, we all know that. She was jealous of Arabella, and the baby on the way made it ten times worse. A divorce would hit her vanity and her pocket. She had the opportunity to do it.'

'It's not exactly material evidence.' Dougal rubbed his eyes. 'Even the opportunity wouldn't stand up in court. No one saw her out of the house. Yorick and Newley can't confirm they tried to ring her. The diary and what Tolby said Newley said aren't much use. Take those away and all you're left with is psychological value judgements. Was Tolby even in the same room when Newley used the phone?'

'No. They were in a restaurant, he said, and the payphone was out near the toilets — '

'So it's all hearsay, isn't it? You can't even prove that Newley used the phone.'

'So you don't believe she did it? Come off it.'

Dougal lit another cigarette. If he didn't smoke, he drank more: if he didn't drink he smoked more.

'I didn't say that. Of course she did it. But we can't prove it. The police need facts. Like fingerprints on the murder weapon. Eye witnesses. You know the sort of thing. I imagine they're even more necessary when the person concerned is an old friend of the Assistant Commissioner's wife.'

Even the corpse was no longer available, since Arabella had been cremated. That was something he could hardly mention to Lorton. The whole business was a tangle of supposition. The one solid fact was that Newley was dead. For all Dougal knew he was sitting opposite the murderer. He wondered how solid the fact still was: decomposition in water must produce strange results.

'The weather forecast mentioned a thaw,' Dougal said. 'By next weekend, if not sooner.'

'Come again?'

'Warmer weather. Spring. Sunshine.' Dougal didn't bother to keep the sarcasm out of his voice. Fear often made him sarcastic; he had noticed that before. 'Ice melts. Things come to the surface.'

Lorton shrugged. 'It'll have to happen sooner or later. At least he's had a bit of time in there. That'll make things easier.'

Gloves waving in the water . . .

'When they find Newley,' Dougal said softly, 'there'll be a manhunt. No one's going to claim *that's* an accident.'

'Okay, there'll be a fuss. We can just sit tight.'

Dougal shook his head. 'I don't like it. Don't forget the police are already interested in you.'

The old fear lurked at the back of his mind: suppose Lorton had set him up for Newley's murder? Concealing the body might have delayed the scheme, but not aborted it.

'Got any ideas?' Lorton said. 'You're the R-and-D man.'

'Just a small one,' Dougal said. He ran it through his mind. It should fulfil the double function of protecting himself and appealing to Lorton. He thought it could work.

Lorton tapped the side of his glass. 'Let's have it.'

'How about if we tell the police where Newley is?'

'Oh, for God's sake — '

'I haven't finished,' Dougal snapped. For an instant he savoured his temporary possession of the whip hand. 'We tell the police where the body is. And we give them a murderer to go with it.'

Chapter 16

'RUBBISH!' GEORGINA SAID. 'You both took at least ninety minutes for lunch. I timed you myself.'

'We got stuck in a queue,' Fiona said. 'We'll make up the time, I promise.'

'It's not good enough. It's not just your time-keeping that concerns me.' Georgina turned on Zaza. 'It may interest you to know that I've just had Mr Standish on the phone. He was wondering why I hadn't returned his call. Understandably he was very annoyed. So am I. Well?'

Zaza's lower lip trembled ominously.

'I cannot and will not tolerate incompetence. This is the second time you've failed to pass on a *vital* message. And as for you, Fiona, words fail me.' Georgina picked up a letter from her desk, screwed it up and threw it at the waste-paper basket. 'How my husband put up with you for so long I just don't know. You call yourself a trained secretary?'

'But there was only one mistake in that letter, Mrs Newley,' Fiona said; she was made of slightly sterner stuff than Zaza. 'I'm sure no one would have noticed — '

'I noticed. And it was your third attempt, too.' Georgina pulled off her coat and flung it on the chair. 'As a matter of fact, it's your last attempt. You're both fired. I want the pair of you out of the office in ten minutes. Do I make myself clear?'

Zaza began to weep. Fiona tried to negotiate about wages in lieu of notice.

'Hugo will see to that sort of thing,' Georgina said. 'By post. Now get out of my sight.'

The two girls fled. Celia and Brassard, who had overheard everything from the outer office, exchanged rueful glances. NCPR's corps of secretaries was now down to one woman, a middle-aged Italian with a moustache. Brassard murmured that the moustache had saved Angelica's job. Like Celia, he suspected that Georgina's chief objection to the other secretaries was not their undoubted lack of efficiency but the fact that they were young and pretty.

Georgina emerged from her room. Brassard's phone began to ring; he seized the opportunity to escape.

'You'd better organize a couple of temps for us,' Georgina said.

Celia looked at her watch. 'It'll have to be tomorrow. The agency'll be closing — it's nearly half-past five.'

'We'll advertize for permanent replacements, I think.'

Georgina chatted for a few minutes about the qualities she considered desirable in a secretary; she even asked Celia's opinion. By handing in her notice, Celia had somehow increased her standing at NCPR. Georgina's civility made her feel queasy.

In the background she could hear Brassard being soothing on the phone: 'Of course, Ron . . . No problem . . . Yes, I know today's Tuesday . . . Just leave it with me . . . Only too glad to help . . .'

But when he put down the phone, he was wearing what Celia called his crisis face. That in itself was not unusual. Public relations, she sometimes thought, could be defined as a series of crises created by other people.

'Oh God,' he moaned.

'What is it?' Georgina said.

Brassard waved at the phone. 'That was Ron. You know he's editing *The Silicon Leisure Review* now? They're due to go to press this evening and someone's failed to meet the deadline. He needs a fifteen-hundred word article by eight-thirty at the latest. I said I'd do it.'

'Splendid,' Georgina said. 'We'll leave you to it.'

'That's just it. I owe him a favour, so I couldn't say no. But it means I'll have to cancel the meeting with Clive.'

'You can't do that,' Georgina said firmly. 'We need the account.'

Both of them looked at Celia. She knew what was coming. She also knew that, if she refused, the crisis would turn into a five-act melodrama.

'All right,' she said, before they could ask. 'Don't worry. I'll do it.'

Celia's motives for volunteering were not entirely altruistic. If she ever went freelance, she would need all the contacts she could get.

She had nothing planned for the evening. She rang William to tell him she would be late. To her surprise he offered to come over to the office. As Brassard was leaving, he warned the security man at the front entrance that Celia was expecting a visitor.

The article itself was easy enough. The only editorial guideline was that the subject should have something to do with leisure software for home computers. It was a superb opportunity to enthuse about RTI's products. There was no need to worry about her lack of knowledge: public relations trained you to write authoritatively about everything from tractors to lingerie.

Her raw material came from RTI's press releases and from other people's articles in previous issues of *The Silicon Leisure Review*. She cobbled together a rough draft and then rewrote it, trying to remove the more ostentatious signs of plagiarism.

The contract cleaners hoovered and dusted around her. They left at seven o'clock, as Celia was starting her third draft. Though she had never admitted it to anyone, she disliked being alone in the office since Arabella had fallen to her death from the fire escape: and the feeling was always worse in the evening.

William arrived promptly at half-past seven. She greeted him with a smile, hoping her relief wasn't too obvious.

'How's it going?' he asked.

'I won't be long. Ten or fifteen minutes.'

William was carrying a briefcase. 'I brought the first sixty pages of *Fallen Angel*.'

'That'll please Georgina.' Celia rolled another sheet of paper into the typewriter.

'I hope she likes my invoice too. I'll leave it in her in-tray, shall I?'

'As you like.' Celia made two typing errors in the next sentence. William's readiness to make money out of Yorick still seemed rather tasteless. She ripped out the paper and put in a fresh sheet.

She had done another paragraph before it occurred to her that he was taking a long time in Georgina's office. She swivelled round in her chair. William had a manilla envelope in his hand. He slid it into his briefcase.

'What are you doing?'

Celia wished she could take back the words. She was getting too suspicious these days.

William snapped shut the lock. 'I've taken another envelope: it'll do for the next batch of typescript.' He walked towards her. 'You don't mind, do you? Or does it count as petty thieving?'

His voice was light, but she thought she detected an undercurrent of bitterness.

'Of course not.' She turned back to the typewriter to avoid looking at his face. 'I just wondered, that's all.'

William read through the article, finding two literals, while she finished the last page. Celia corrected the mistakes with a pen. If Georgina had been here, she would have insisted on having both pages retyped. William photocopied it for her while she addressed an envelope.

She fetched her coat. When she got back, she found William standing by the open door of the fire escape. Cold air eddied around her. She shivered as she buttoned up her coat.

'I've been using the front entrance lately.'

'I know.' William smiled at her. 'But this is quicker. Let's go and face the ghosts together.'

Lorton watched Dougal surreptitiously as they walked along the path through the woods. He knew that Dougal was equally wary of him.

They walked in silence. The ground was still hard, despite the thaw, and they left no traces. Beyond the bare, black branches of the trees, the sky was a harsh and brilliant blue.

There was no real need for both of them to be here. But it had been accepted from the start, without the need for discussion, that this would be a joint expedition. It was the inevitable corollary of the absence of trust between them.

The hire car was down in the car park, the one near Miller's End. Dougal was worried that someone might see it; but Lorton thought that unlikely. A Wednesday morning in winter wasn't likely to attract tourists or walkers. Miller's End was empty, and no one but a stray farm-worker was going to use the lane. And why should anyone bother to make a note of the car's number? It was a chance worth taking.

They came to the track which ran along the spine of the ridge. There were fresh horse-droppings on the beaten earth. Dougal looked from left to right, then left again, like a child on the edge of a busy road.

'We go straight on,' Lorton said.

Dougal nodded.

'Cheer up,' Lorton suggested. 'It may never happen.'

'I should tell you,' Dougal mumbled. 'I left a letter with my solicitor, to be opened by him if I don't reclaim it within a certain time.'

Lorton glanced sharply at him and then burst out laughing.

'It's not funny.'

'Keep your hair on.' Lorton grinned. 'For all I know you're planning to pin it on me. How do I know you didn't top Newley yourself?'

Dougal shrugged. 'Do I look the type?'

'There isn't a type.'

Their eyes met, and they smiled. The smiles were cautious, expecting rebuffs. They emerged into the clearing. The weather-stained dome of the gazebo faced them. Beside it was the pond. Someone had rolled a tyre into the middle of it.

'The ice is still holding,' Lorton said. 'Where did you . . . ?'

Dougal pointed to the spot immediately alongside the gazebo. 'In about three feet of water.'

They spoke in whispers. Around them the trees were silent: the day was windless, and the birds weren't on speaking terms with one another.

Lorton cleared his throat. 'We'll be able to hear if anyone comes. It's so bloody quiet here. Give me a city any day.'

Dougal nosed around the clearing while Lorton watched.

'I probably made that mark on the ground when I pulled over the door . . . there's a scrape on the floor of the gazebo . . . must have happened when I pushed him over.'

'Nothing to worry about. You going to be all day? I'm cold.' Lorton unzipped his coat and pulled out the envelope. 'Where do we put them?'

'One of the tissues could go down here, between the grass and the base of the gazebo.' Dougal crouched down to show him. 'We'll have to give it a few days to get properly weather-beaten. We could shove the other one in the wreck of the old car.'

'Bit obvious, ain't it?'

Dougal straightened up. 'If you've got a better idea, why don't you say so?'

'All right, sorry I spoke. What about the hairs?'

'I thought perhaps on the gazebo itself. Somewhere out of the wind. I'm sure they'll look there.' Dougal frowned. 'What are you doing?'

Lorton had jumped up on the gazebo. He ran his gloved hand along the shelf above the pillars. He winked at Dougal.

'Just thought I'd check. That ten thousand quid must be somewhere.'

'Well it's not there,' Dougal said. He looked thoughtfully at Lorton. 'Nor's the Jacobite Guinea.'

The week crawled by. Dougal tried to immerse himself in *The Journal of a Fallen Angel*. As time went by, he made fewer and fewer corrections. It was easier to act merely as a copy-typist: the thumping of the keys deadened the mind.

He was sleeping badly, and he knew Celia was worried about him. He made pressure of work into an excuse for not seeing as much of her as usual. Typing five or six thousand words of drivel every day was a strange way to keep sane.

The next job was his alone. He considered going into an office equipment shop, as Lorton had done. In the event, however, he bought a secondhand typewriter at a street market and a pad of cheap paper from Woolworth's.

The message was very simple: IVOR NEWLEY WAS MURDERED BY HIS WIFE. HE'S IN THE POND NEAR THEIR COTTAGE. He addressed the envelope to the Chief Constable of Hampshire.

Dougal allowed himself no frills, like misspellings or too much information. He carried caution to absurd lengths. He defaced the typewriter keys with a file and made a special trip to Hertfordshire to drop it in a reservoir. Drowning the typewriter reminded him of what he had done to the remains of Ivor Newley.

Celia was working at the office on Saturday morning. Dougal brought the letter to Lorton, who read it and sealed it. They took a bus to Regent Street and posted the letter at the Heddon Street post office.

Lorton suggested going for a drink, but Dougal refused. His alcohol-free time zone still had twelve hours more to run. And he didn't feel like celebrating.

The police came just before lunch on the following Wednesday.

Celia was on the phone to Jeremy Murgatroyd. They were discussing the launch of a new range of low-calorie snacks. Murgatroyd wanted to change the basis of the launch at the last moment: he had the idea of claiming that he had found instructions for making the snacks in a recipe book compiled by his great-grandmother. He was a tenacious man, and it was difficult to dissuade him.

Maxham was the first to appear; Celia recognized him from his previous visits to the office. He was accompanied by another, taller man and by a sturdy WPC with dyed blonde hair.

'Look, Jeremy,' Celia said for the second time. 'I don't think the Victorians had heard of peanut butter. Or calories, for that matter.'

In the reception area, Angelica gestured at the closed door of Georgina's office. 'But I can't interrupt her. She'll kill me.'

'Why not?' Murgatroyd demanded. 'Peanut butter must have been invented. And we needn't call them calories — we could just say the recipes were "suitable for ladies on a reducing diet" or something like that.'

Angelica gave way. Maxham led his colleagues through the office. Angelica, still protesting, trailed behind them.

Celia sighed. 'But it's such a hackneyed gimmick — '

'Tell you what.' There was a burst of enthusiasm on the other end of the line. 'We could say great-granny was American. Then we could use a *Gone with the Wind* angle in the advertising. I suppose it's too late to put an antebellum mansion on the label?'

'It's too late to change *anything*,' Celia said firmly. 'I have to go. I'll ring you tomorrow.'

Maxham knocked once on Georgina's door and opened it. The police filed into the office. A moment later the beautiful young man from Gasset and Lode came out, looking peeved. The door closed behind him.

Celia beckoned to Angelica. 'What's it all about?'

Angelica shrugged. 'How should I know?' she whispered. 'But the tall one's a Superintendent.'

They were not kept in suspense for more than five minutes. The door opened, and Georgina came out with the police. The WPC helped her into the mink.

'Thank you *so* much.' Georgina turned to Celia. 'Tell Hugo I've gone out, will you? The police need my help. I'm not sure when I'll be back.'

Chapter 17

CELIA WROTE A letter shortly before the trial started.

> *Dear Georgina*
> *I'm terribly sorry about all this. Would you like me to visit you, if that's possible? And is there anything I can bring or send you?*
> *With best wishes,*
>   *Celia.*

It was a difficult letter to write, and probably an unsatisfactory one to receive. Celia disliked Georgina intensely, and she had little doubt of her guilt. But Georgina had been kind to her, in her own way. She had no living relatives and, so far as Celia was aware, none of her friendships had survived her arrest. Someone had to write.

Celia told no one but William. He shrugged and said that he loved her, which was reassuring to hear if not particularly helpful.

To Celia's relief, Georgina did not answer the letter.

Georgina Newley was charged with the murder of her husband.

Lorton noticed that the news appeared to give pleasure to a great many people. Georgina had never been well-liked. Nor had Ivor; but the circumstances of his death gave him a posthumous popularity, if only to make the crime of which Georgina was accused seem fouler. The Newleys' acquaintances spoke well of the dead in order to think ill of the living.

Lorton followed the case in the press. He would have liked to have watched it from the public gallery; but that would have been asking for trouble. Besides, he had enough to do at home, now the house was on the market at last.

Georgina pleaded not guilty. As the trial progressed, and the evidence mounted up, it became increasingly difficult to take the plea seriously. She made matters worse by her hauteur in court. On one occasion she called the judge 'you silly old man'. She was apt to accuse the witnesses for the prosecution of lying.

The pieces of evidence fell into place with the unequivocal precision of a well-made jigsaw puzzle. Ivor Newley had last been seen alive by independent witnesses on the morning of Sunday, 27 January. He had been killed, either on the same day or shortly afterwards; and the murderer had dumped his body in the pond near the Newleys' country cottage in Hampshire. The weapon, a kitchen knife which probably came from Miller's End, had been found when the police dragged the pond. It was assumed, reasonably enough, that the murder had taken place in or near the gazebo by the pond, because of the difficulty of moving a heavy body.

The prosecution argued that the Newleys had driven down together from London; after the murder, Mrs Newley had driven back in her husband's car, and parked it near their home; no doubt she hoped that the trip to Hampshire would never come to light.

The deceased's solicitor, Eustace Tolby, attested that Newley was on the verge of instituting divorce proceedings against his wife. Mrs Newley was bitterly opposed to the idea, for financial and emotional reasons. No one actually said that she was a jealous, greedy woman; it was implied sufficiently clearly by the facts. She stood to gain substantially from her husband's death, since he had not made a will.

Hugo Brassard confirmed with obvious reluctance that Georgina Newley had lost no time in taking control of her husband's business after his disappearance. Her domineering managerial techniques must have prejudiced the jury against her still more.

Since Georgina denied that she had been to Miller's End since Christmas, and to the woods behind the cottage since the previous autumn, the forensic evidence clinched the case against her. Hairs from her mink coat had been found in the

166

gazebo by the pond. Two tissues discovered in the vicinity showed traces of her mucus and her saliva.

No one mentioned Arabella. Georgina kept quiet about her because she had the wit to see that knowledge of the affair would strengthen her motive for killing her husband, at least in the eyes of the jury. Celia and Dougal said nothing, partly because they weren't asked. Lorton said nothing because he couldn't bear to bring Arabella into it. Tolby said nothing about Arabella because Lorton threatened to break his neck if he did.

On the last day the jury was out for thirty minutes. They decided unanimously that Georgina Newley was guilty. The judge gave her a life sentence.

As the court rose, Georgina shouted: 'I'm not guilty!'

On the evening of the same day, Hugo Brassard invited Celia to dinner. They went to a Greek restaurant in Charlotte Street. Brassard had a liking for retsina, fostered by his annual package holiday to Greece.

While they nibbled their way through the starters, Brassard talked about the Elgin Marbles, the traffic problem in Athens and the best way of making houmus. His voice was low and urgent, as if he was talking about something completely different. Celia made monosyllabic replies. Her stomach felt uneasy. She blamed it on the after-effects of the trial and the feta cheese in the salad.

Brassard was looking drawn, and the nervous movements of his limbs were more pronounced than usual. Though the trial was over, the strain of the last few weeks was still affecting both of them.

Celia's patience snapped when he poured her the second glass of retsina.

'Hugo, can't we stop pretending everything's normal? You didn't ask me here to talk about your summer holidays.'

'No, you're right.' Brassard pushed aside his plate. 'Um . . . I should have said this earlier: I did appreciate you withdrawing your notice.'

'It wasn't particularly virtuous. Georgina was my main reason for leaving in the first place.'

'I know. All the same, most people would have been all too glad to get off the sinking ship. Which makes it such a pity . . .'

'What are you trying to say?'

Brassard rested his elbows on the table and leant forward. 'The ship's sunk, I'm afraid.'

'NCPR?'

'You must have guessed. The firm won't survive this sort of scandal. Arabella's death was bad enough, but this is ten times worse. Half our clients have already told us they won't renew their contracts. Can't say I blame them.'

'What about the legal position?'

'Complicated.' Brassard fiddled with a piece of pitta bread. 'But that's not the point. As far as PR's concerned, the Newleys are the kiss of death.' He flushed. 'Sorry. But you know what I mean.'

Celia nodded. She had a fair idea of what was coming.

'I was wondering,' Brassard confided to his wine glass, 'whether you'd be interested in joining me in a new agency. As a partner, that is. A fresh start, eh?'

'It's worth thinking about,' Celia said. 'But you do realize I haven't much capital?'

Brassard twitched. 'Money isn't everything. I think you'd bring two clients with you, possibly more. Henry Magus and that odious Jeremy Murgatroyd, for certain. And perhaps RTI: I happen to know that Joe's been very impressed with your work. That article you wrote went down very well. Um . . . a couple of my own clients will stay loyal. And I think I could persuade my bank manager to give us a loan.'

'We'd have to find an office,' Celia said. 'And staff — '

'I know of a short lease up for sale, just off Soho Square,' Brassard interrupted. 'You're right about an office: people always think you're a Mickey Mouse outfit if you work from home. But we needn't worry too much about staff. I always thought NCPR had employed too many people. We could get a word-processor and do most of our own typing. We could always farm things out to freelances. Everyone uses freelances these days. No national insurance, no office space, no fringe benefits: they're cost-effective.'

'I'm definitely interested.' Celia incautiously swallowed a mouthful of retsina. 'I wonder if we should ask . . .'

Her voice trailed away, and she shuddered. The wine was sour in her mouth. Her stomach heaved. All she could think of was pine-scented engine oil and the need to get it out of her system.

'Are you all right?' Brassard asked.

'No,' Celia said. 'I think I'm going to be sick.'

'How soon could you be out?'

'By next week, if you wanted,' Lorton said.

Mr Bentley lingered in the hall, surreptitiously examining the state of the decoration. He was a plump man who looked as if he would burst if you sat on him. His wife had asked to use the bathroom, presumably to test the plumbing.

'You've got a lodger, haven't you?'

'No problem there. She's already fixed up.'

'Of course I'd like to see the house by daylight before we make up our minds. But I don't mind saying we're very interested. Very interested indeed.'

Three other people had also said they were interested in the last few days. But none of them had been interested enough to come up with an offer.

Mrs Bentley appeared at the head of the stairs. 'I do like the banisters. They're an original feature, aren't they?'

'Of course. So are the downstairs fireplaces.'

Bentley cleared his throat. 'I should make it quite clear that speed's important for us. If we did go ahead, we'd like to exchange as soon as possible. We've already sold our house in Manchester. The firm's paying for a rented flat but it's not really big enough for us and the children.'

'They're away at school at present,' the woman said. 'But they'll be home at Easter. Do you have any children?'

Lorton shook his head.

'I hope you don't mind me asking,' she continued, 'but one has to ask, doesn't one? Why are you moving? It's such a delightful house.'

'It's too big for one person. My wife died a few months ago.' Lorton saw the mixture of embarrassment and doubt on the woman's fat, powdered face. 'She didn't die here. She fell off the office fire escape.'

The husband glanced desperately at the front door. 'Sorry to hear that . . . We must be off, dear. We'll be in touch, Mr Lorton.'

Lorton showed them out and went to the kitchen to pour himself a drink. The Bentleys were the tenth set of prospective purchasers whom he had shown round the house. Some of them were politer than others, but they tended to ask the same questions as they trampled through the house. It was wearing work.

The door bell rang again. Lorton looked up at the clock: Dougal was due at nine-thirty, but it was only nine. He recapped the whisky bottle and left it on the table.

Detective Sergeant Maxham was standing on the doorstep. His grey hair was shiny with rain. He was alone.

'What do you want?' Lorton didn't trouble to make his voice civil.

'Just a word.' Maxham edged into the hall, smiling his salesman's smile. 'You by yourself tonight?'

Lorton nodded. It occurred to him, out of the blue, that Maxham was physically inconsistent: the fleshy face didn't fit the skinny body. The incongruity disturbed him.

'You've done a nice job here.' Maxham looked along the hall and up the stairs. 'My old woman is house-hunting: she'd like this. Classy. Myself, I can't see what's wrong with Croydon. But she's right about one thing: we do need a bigger house. But where's the cash going to come from, that's what I want to know. I wish she had the answer to that.'

'Where's your mate?' Lorton said. 'You know, the panda who keeps an eye on my drinking habits.'

'Bernie's off-duty. So am I, as a matter of fact. This isn't really an official visit.' Maxham's pale-blue eyes glanced down the hall to the kitchen. The whisky bottle was in full view. 'Celebrating? I thought you might be.'

'I don't know what you mean.'

Maxham affected surprise. 'You haven't heard the news? About the trial?'

'Of course I have. What's that got to do with it?'

'Nice little case,' Maxham said, as if that was a cause for celebration. 'A body. A killer. An open-shut trial, and the judge congratulates the police on their brilliant investigation. Everyone pats themselves on the back and goes home.'

'Except you.' Lorton looked at his watch. He didn't want Dougal to run into Maxham. On the other hand, he needed to know what the man was up to. 'I've got someone coming to look at the house in ten minutes.'

'Except me,' Maxham agreed. 'I wouldn't say no to a small scotch, seeing as I'm off-duty.'

'I'll give you two minutes.'

Lorton led the way into the kitchen and poured them both a drink. Maxham leant against the sink, glass in hand, and sighed with pleasure. Lorton sat down at the table.

'It wasn't my case any longer,' Maxham said. 'I sometimes think regional CIDs can get a bit parochial in their thinking. Don't always see the wider picture. I mean, none of them seemed too worried about that anonymous letter. I'd want to know who sent it. And why. But no: the Hampshire boys had this ready-made killer, so they didn't bother about anyone else.'

'I wouldn't worry too much, if I were you,' Lorton said. 'I expect whoever sent that letter just didn't want to get involved.'

Maxham sipped his drink and smacked his lips appreciatively.

'It's a malt, ain't it? Quite a treat for me.' He blinked rapidly. 'You know, if anyone had asked me — and no one did, mind you — I'd have said that several people had a reason to kill Newley. I'd have been happier if someone had actually seen the woman down there over the weekend. A farmer said he saw a car down his lane on the Sunday night — just a pair of headlights, he thought it was a courting couple; but that was on the other side of the ridge, away from Miller's End.'

'Maybe he was right. About the courting couple.'

'Maybe.' Maxham stared up at the ceiling. 'There were a few loose ends. What do you think happened to that ten thousand quid?'

'Georgina must have got it.'

Maxham shrugged. 'We found no trace of it. Perhaps she hid it. A little nest-egg for her old age.'

'You said loose ends.' Lorton waited for a moment. 'What else was there?'

'A few odds and sods. I had a look at Newley's papers. Do you know, just before he vanished, he'd written to Custodemus: he wanted to update his home security. *Very* wise. But I wonder why. He hadn't reported a burglary. That's when most people start worrying. Another thing: the house is in Mrs Newley's name. But he was just about to walk out. So why was he worrying about burglar alarms for her?'

'Maybe he still felt responsible for her. Some couples go on like that, even after they're divorced.'

'You think the Newleys were like that?' Maxham chuckled. 'Well, you should know, Mr Lorton, having worked with them. And of course you knew them socially too. But you weren't at the Newleys' party, were you? Must have been the weekend before he died. No, of course not. But I expect Miss Prentisse told you about it. Some practical joker rang up: said there was a gas leak, and they had to evacuate the house.'

Lorton shrugged. 'Some people have a weird sense of humour.'

Maxham drained his glass and put it in the sink. 'You're right there. Take Fred Mahony, for instance. You know — little bloke, plays a lot of pool. Bernie said he saw you together. Always joking about rats: that's what I call a weird sense of humour. I heard a whisper that he's been selling coins lately. Newley collected coins. Funny little coincidence, eh?'

'What coincidence?'

'Why — that you knew them both.'

Lorton glanced at his watch. 'You'll have to go now.'

'All good things must end, Mr Lorton. That's what I tell my old woman. Don't get up. I'll see myself out.' Maxham winced as he walked across the kitchen. 'The verruca's bad tonight. I reckon it needs surgery. If I could afford it, I'd go private.'

'These days it's all a question of money,' Lorton said.

'Everything has its price. I'm all for the free market

economy.' Maxham hobbled into the hall. 'Thanks for the drink. I'll be in touch.'

'I feel perfectly all right now,' Celia said. 'I don't know why Hugo bothered with a taxi. What on earth's that?'

'Black tea with a bit of sugar.' Dougal sat on the edge of the bed and smiled at her. 'I rather like mothering you. What do you think caused it?'

'The smell of that cheese. I'm sure it was off. I've been feeling delicate all day, what with the trial and everything. I can't help wondering how Georgina's feeling. It's all such a *waste*.'

Dougal squeezed her hand. 'You wouldn't want her to get away scot-free.'

'That's not what I mean.' Celia pulled away from him. 'I know she's a killer. But it must be terrible to be so alone.'

'Let's change the subject. Are you going to accept Hugo's offer?'

'I think so. I have to do something. And I trust Hugo.'

She lay back on the pillows. Dougal caught sight of the clock: it was nearly ten. He had missed his appointment with Lorton.

Celia stirred. 'Do you still want a lodger?'

It took him a moment to realize what she meant. 'Yes, please.'

She began to brush her hair. 'I have to move out soon,' she said quickly. 'It's not fair to Rod. He wants a quick sale. I think half the people who've come to see the house suspect I'm a sitting tenant.'

'I'll hire a van this weekend, if you like,' Dougal said casually. 'Saturday suit you?'

Celia's arm came round him. The cup of tea fell to the carpet. A minute later, Dougal tried to pull away. But Celia pinned him down.

'I told you,' she said. 'I feel fine now.'

Dougal no longer dreamed of skin gloves waving in the water. He had a new dream, now, in which he was chased by something or someone down the long, windowless corridors of an institutional building. He never saw his pursuer, though occasionally he heard it snuffling behind him.

Now and then a door slammed, sending metallic echoes rolling along the corridors. There must be a door to the outside world: it was only a matter of time before he found it. The problem was, he didn't have any time.

The trial was over. He should have all the time in the world. But it wasn't as simple as that. Part of him still found it difficult to forget what he had done to Georgina Newley. It was profoundly humiliating that his dreaming mind still owed allegiance to a rudimentary conscience. Dougal had officially dismissed his conscience when he was in his teens.

The morning after the trial he woke up soaked with sweat. Celia slept peacefully beside him. It was only six o'clock, but he decided to get up.

He pulled on his clothes and stumbled into the kitchen. He could hear Lorton moving around quietly on the floor above. He remembered he had missed their appointment last night. They would have to meet sooner or later.

Lorton was in the room which had been Arabella's studio. He was doing press-ups, an activity which Dougal found distasteful.

Lorton raised himself as far as he could. 'You couldn't sleep either?'

Dougal shook his head. He wandered into the kitchen, where he found a freshly-brewed pot of tea. He poured himself a cup and lit a cigarette. Lorton followed him. He was wearing a red tracksuit, and his breathing was normal.

'You didn't turn up last night.'

'I got diverted,' Dougal said. 'By the way, Celia's moving out on Saturday.'

'Good.'

'Hugo Brassard's asked her to join him in a new agency. She wondered if you wanted to come in too.'

Lorton shook his head. 'I've got other plans.'

Dougal flicked ash into the sink. 'I brought the rest of the coins. Do you think it's safe to sell them as a job lot?'

'I changed my mind,' Lorton said. 'You can keep them. They're all yours.'

'But why?'

'I had a caller last night. Sergeant Maxham. He's worried about the loose ends in the Newley case.'

'Surely it's all over now?' Dougal's fingers tightened involuntarily, denting the cigarette. 'What loose ends?'

'Don't worry. You're not involved. Yet.' The words were like a slap in the face.

'But what's he got to go on?'

'Nothing to worry you.' Lorton smiled. 'He doesn't want to nick me, you know. He just wants to blackmail me.'

Chapter 18

'FOWLER-TROON?' BRASSARD SAID. 'I remember: rather a Colonel Blimp, if you ask me.' He drummed his fingers on the top of the desk and frowned. 'Hardly a possible client. Are you sure you can spare the time?'

'Of course I can,' Celia said firmly. 'You can have my sandwiches if you want. You know where they are.'

She left the tiny office at once, knowing it was unlikely that she would find a better exit line. Her sandwiches were in the bottom drawer of her desk, as Brassard was well aware. The move from NCPR had lessened the scope for his prying but he had increased, by way of compensation, its depth of penetration.

Working in close proximity to Hugo had its disadvantages. She had discovered that the only way to cope was to be firm with him. He had a tendency to forget that she was an equal partner now, not an employee.

It was a bright morning in April. For the first time this year, Celia was prepared to concede that spring was a serious possibility. She walked down Greek Street, noticing that several people had been hardy enough to come out in their shirt-sleeves. The passers-by seemed unusually cheerful. Celia caught the mood: there were still problems to be faced but at least the dreadful winter was past.

She turned into Old Compton Street. The windows of Daudet's sparkled in the sunshine. She climbed the stairs and was greeted effusively by the head waiter. He ushered her to Fowler-Troon's usual table.

The Brigadier half-rose to his feet. 'How are you, my dear?' he boomed. 'You're looking well.'

Celia smiled at him. 'It must be the new job. Though self-employment can be a bit harrowing at times.'

'A lot to be said for being your own master. Better than

working for Ivor Newley, eh? Poor chap, of course.' Fowler-Troon, perhaps aware that his remark was not in the best of taste, cast around for another subject. 'Had an awful job getting hold of you.'

'We're not in the phone book yet. And I moved flats while you were away. I'm in Kilburn now.' Celia, grateful for the ambiguities permitted by the English language, added that she was sharing with a friend.

'Kilburn?' Fowler-Troon said, a shade too loudly. 'Don't think I know anyone who actually lives there.'

Celia ignored her host's surprise. 'How was Australia? It's given you a lovely tan.'

'Well. Put it this way: Australia's a young country and I'm an old man.' He shook his head. 'My daughter wanted me to try surfing. Wine's awful but I rather took to the lager.'

The waiter hovered beside their table. They took refuge in their menus. There was good will on both sides, Celia thought, but not a lot to say.

The conversation faltered during the meal. The patches of silence lengthened. They reached the coffee stage. Celia asked for tea.

'Not on some diet, are you?' Fowler-Troon said. 'Everyone seems to have their own fad, these days.'

Celia shook her head. 'Just a whim.' Coffee gave her indigestion at present, but her host would probably think indigestion was faddy as well.

'I can eat anything. Know what I attribute that to? Curry. Have lots of curry when you're young, that's my advice. It strengthens the insides for life.' Fowler-Troon glanced at his watch, sucked in his breath and said, in a lower voice: 'I've got a little problem. I'd appreciate your advice.'

He sat back in his chair with the self-satisfied look of a swimmer who had finally plucked up the courage to dive, only to find that the water wasn't as cold as he had expected. Celia tried to look intelligent, sympathetic and encouraging.

'It's this Newley business. I saw nothing about it in Australia. Someone mentioned it to me when I got back, another collector. Came as a complete shock.'

'Everything happened very quickly,' Celia said.

'Very unpleasant. Still, you can't say I didn't warn you. That's one thing I told myself: at least I did my best for Richard's girl.' The glow of self-congratulation on Fowler-Troon's face faded rapidly. 'But it does leave me in a rather awkward position.'

'Why?'

'You remember that valuation I did for Mrs Newley? Just before I went to Australia?' Fowler-Troon fumbled in his waistcoat pocket. 'I found this.'

He placed a small transparent wallet on the table between them. It contained a thin, golden disc. Fowler-Troon touched the edge of the wallet with the tip of a finger.

'Jacobus III,' he said reverently. 'Dei Gratia, Magnae Britanniae, Franciae et Hiberniae Rex. 1744. The Royal Stuart arms.'

'So you were right.'

'Only about the Jacobite Guinea. Everything else in the collection seemed to have been legitimately acquired. There were receipts, and so forth.'

'Did you tell Mrs Newley?'

Fowler-Troon avoided her eyes. 'Extraordinary woman . . . I was going to tell her but I decided in the end that it would be best to have a word with Newley himself. Of course I didn't know that he was dead. I'm afraid I stalled — said I needed to get a second opinion on one of the coins. I . . . I had to hint I might be interested in buying it myself.'

He sipped his coffee. Celia could sense his distress. The avarice of a collector was at war with his conscience.

'So the problem is, who owns it?'

Fowler-Troon shrugged. 'Newley acquired it dishonestly. He's dead, and I suppose his wife isn't in a position to inherit anything of his.'

'If it belongs to anyone, surely it's to the old lady in Berthing.'

'Mrs Harvey. Yes. But if I return it to her, Mrs Newley might . . . well, turn nasty.'

'I doubt if she could do anything about it. You could always cover yourself by getting your solicitor to write to hers, explaining everything. If you like, I can find out who her solicitor is.'

'You make it sound so simple.' Fowler-Troon sighed. 'It seems such a pity. You see, Mrs Harvey doesn't really appreciate its importance.'

'You never know,' Celia said kindly. 'Perhaps she'll sell it to you.'

The flat in Kilburn had shrunk since Celia moved in.

William seemed content to exist with far fewer possessions than most people required. When he was living there alone, the flat had a spartan air, like the encampment of an impoverished nomad. Now it resembled an overcrowded charity shop.

Celia thought they needed somewhere larger. But she hadn't suggested it because of all the implicit ramifications. For a start, they would have to wait until she had an income worthy of the name. It was unlikely that anyone would give William a larger mortgage; it was something of a miracle that he had got one on the present flat.

The other consideration was more important. At present, living in the same flat, even sharing the same bed, could be interpreted as a casual arrangement, a matter of convenience on both sides. Moving somewhere else, together, would represent a significant commitment to each other. Celia was in favour of that; but she didn't know how William felt. She was tempted to ask him outright, but a suspicion had stopped her. The extent of the commitment might be rather larger than either of them had anticipated. She didn't want to lay herself open to an accusation of emotional blackmail.

When she arrived back, she found him busy in the kitchen. He had been out of work since finishing *The Journal of a Fallen Angel*: consequently he was doing most of the cooking. He was stuffing cannelloni with breadcrumbs and mushrooms, and working his way through a bottle of Bulgarian wine.

He offered her a glass but she shook her head, partly on the principle that her abstinence might set him a good example.

'I don't blame you,' William said, misunderstanding her motive. 'It's awful.'

'Then why drink it?'

'Habit?' he said thoughtfully. 'Natural degeneracy? Latent masochism? The real reason's that I can't afford anything else. I've done a salad to go with this. Shall I do some potatoes too?'

Celia shook her head. 'Not for me. I pigged myself at lunch. Went to Daudet's.'

'That's what comes of having your own expense account.'

'I was taken there. Fowler-Troon rang up this morning with one of his impulse invitations.'

'I thought he was in Australia.'

'He'd just come back. The news about the murder came as a complete shock to him.' Celia perched on the edge of the kitchen table and, changing her mind, poured herself a small glass of wine.

William poured cheese sauce over the cannelloni and slid the dish into the oven. 'He wanted a good gossip?'

'Not just that. He had a problem. He's got the Jacobite Guinea.'

'*What?*'

William paused in the act of refilling his glass. Drops of wine slopped on to the Formica top of the table. A few of them splattered against Celia's handbag.

'Sorry.' He went to the sink for a cloth. 'I thought that was lost for ever — if it ever existed.'

His excitement puzzled her for a moment. She sipped her wine and pushed the glass to his side of the table.

'It's disgusting. You can have mine.'

'I'm sure Gilbert Verrall would be interested. The last time I saw him, he was moaning about the lack of authentic Jacobite relics. What will happen to it?'

'The Jacobite Guinea? Fowler-Troon's in agony, but I think he'll give it back to the old lady. Ivor stole it from her, after all.'

William smiled down at her. 'In any case it gives me an excuse to earn a good-conduct mark from Gilbert.'

Celia opened the fridge. Beside the Perrier water was a bottle of champagne. 'What's this for? We're supposed to be broke.'

'I know.' William picked up a tea towel and burnished the cutlery. 'But I've got a proposition to make, and Balkan plonk seemed inappropriate . . . Celia, will you marry me?'

'What name, sir?'

'George Vere-Thompson,' Dougal said. 'That's Thompson with a P.'

A double-barrelled name inspired confidence. For good measure he added an address near Belgrave Square and a price range which started in six figures. He said he was looking for a detached house with at least four bedrooms in the Primrose Hill area.

The woman who was taking his details continued to look as if she would have rather been somewhere else. Dougal was aggrieved. George Vere-Thompson deserved better treatment. A little honest sycophancy would not have come amiss.

It was Saturday morning and, as Dougal had hoped, the estate agent's showroom was crowded with couples in search of desirable residences. The catchment area stretched down from Hampstead to Regent's Park. Dougal was glad that he had taken the precaution of wearing his only suit, a conservatively-cut but undeniably expensive memento of past affluence; he had also visited a hairdresser on his way from Kilburn. It occurred to him that he might be in the same room as people who could fork out half a million pounds for a Georgian house overlooking the Heath. The thought aroused in him an uncomfortable blend of disgust and envy.

A queue was building up behind him. The receptionist sighed and asked, with barely controlled impatience, whether he wanted to view any particular property.

'I found these.' Dougal fanned out three sets of house details on her desk.

'That one's already gone,' she said wearily. 'And I'm afraid the owners of the Eton Avenue house are away this weekend, and they prefer to be there when people come round.'

'I can't manage a weekday,' Dougal said. 'I'm based in Zurich from Monday to Friday.'

She looked searchingly at him for the first time. 'This one,

Steele's Grove, is empty at present. Usually we send someone round with you but we are rather busy today . . . I could let you have the keys, I suppose. You would bring them straight back, wouldn't you?'

'Of course. And perhaps I could make an appointment to view the Eton Avenue house. How about next weekend?'

Dougal made an appointment he had no intention of keeping and signed for the keys of 29 Steele's Grove. The receptionist didn't ask to see identification. Five minutes later he was walking down Eton Avenue, partly sheltered from the rain by Celia's collapsible umbrella. It seemed incongruous: George Vere-Thompson should have a Porsche, or possibly a Ferrari, which he would park insouciantly on double-yellow lines; he wouldn't be obliged to walk in the rain.

It was the first time that Dougal had been to Steele's Grove since the night of the burglary. The Newleys' house was near the end of the cul-de-sac. The estate agent's signboard hung like a flag above the untidy privet hedge. Chickweed flourished in the cracks in the concrete path up to the front door.

Dougal let himself into the house, bolting the door behind him. The atmosphere was damp. The rooms had already been stripped of furniture, though the fitted carpets remained. It was difficult to imagine an untenanted house as someone's home, any more than a corpse as a living body.

He crossed the drawing room. Without the piano and the display cases, the study seemed much larger. The door of the safe was open. Dougal rolled back the carpet where the piano had stood, exposing the parquet flooring. He used a penknife to lever up the block which concealed Newley's cache.

Inside he found a small, oblong package, wrapped in polythene and secured with elastic bands. He opened it and divided the contents among his pockets.

Georgina was a greedy, inquisitive woman. Dougal had banked on that.

Lorton came to Kilburn to say goodbye and was unreasonably upset to find that neither Celia nor Dougal were at home.

He knew he had only himself to blame: he should have phoned first. No doubt they spent their Saturday mornings shopping or doing something equally blameless together. He was briefly envious of the comfort of a shared domestic routine.

He walked back to Kilburn High Road, wondering how on earth he would spend his last six hours in England. It was then that he caught sight of Celia through the open door of a chemist's shop. She was paying for something at the till.

She turned and saw him in the doorway. She made an odd, involuntary movement, almost as if she wanted to run away. Then she smiled and came towards him.

'Hello, Rod. What are you doing here?'

'I've come to say goodbye.'

Celia dropped her purchase into her bag. 'Have you sold the house?'

'We completed yesterday. The Bentleys were in a hurry too.'

Lorton knew he had made a mistake in coming. He hadn't seen Celia since she moved out of his house. In a few weeks they had moved apart, into different lives.

She fingered the strap of her bag. 'What are you going to do?'

'I'm going abroad. South Africa.' He realized from her expression that he had made another mistake. Celia, like Arabella, subscribed to the liberal clichés of the middle classes.

'I would have thought,' she said carefully, 'that South Africa's a bit unstable at present.'

'That's why I'm going. People are pulling out. There's a lot of money to be made if you're willing to take chances.'

'I'm sure there is. I wish you luck.'

'It's for the best, you know.' Lorton had never found Celia more desirable than now. 'I'm not suited to all this.' He waved his arm in a vague gesture which included the crowded pavement where they stood, Arabella's ghost and the city which sprawled around them. Embarrassment made him change the subject: 'How's it going with Hugo?'

'Okay. If we can survive the next six months, I think we'll be all right.'

'And William?'

Her face brightened. 'We're getting married.'

'Congratulations.' He looked away, unsettled by her happiness. 'When's the wedding?'

'We haven't decided. But fairly soon.'

'I'll have to send you a wedding present.' He moved aside, to allow a customer to leave the shop. 'Will you give William a message for me? Just tell him it wasn't me. He'll know what I mean.'

Suddenly Lorton could bear it no longer. He gave her a quick pat on the shoulder and slipped away. She said something as he left. It might have been, 'Rod, take care of yourself.'

The phone rang while she was in the bathroom.

According to the instructions, she should have left what she was doing until the morning; the best time was immediately after getting up. But she was too on edge to wait. If necessary she could always try again.

She felt guilty that she hadn't invited Rod Lorton back to the flat for a cup of coffee. The Kilburn High Road wasn't the best place to say goodbye. But she had been in a hurry to get home, and she needed to be alone for what she wanted to do.

As usual the telephone generated a sense of urgency: it might be something important. But still she lingered in the bathroom.

The procedure reminded her of chemistry experiments at school; all that was missing was the Bunsen burner. You had to wait for two hours before the results became clear. There was a dreadful temptation to spend the interval staring fixedly at what she thought of as the apparatus. It consisted largely of a test tube mounted in a Perspex container, at the base of which was a mirror, set at an angle to the horizontal. The pharmacist had leered at her when she bought it.

The phone was an unwelcome diversion; but at least it gave her something else to think about. She went through to the living-room to answer it.

'May I speak to William Dougal?' It was a man's voice, and it was somehow familiar, though Celia couldn't put a name or a face to it.

'I'm afraid he's out. He should be back this afternoon. Shall I ask him to phone you?'

'Perhaps I could leave a message?' the voice suggested.

'Of course.' Celia found a pencil and some paper among the clutter on the table where William worked. When he worked.

'My name's Gilbert Verrall. William was going to come and see me on Monday morning. Would you ask him if he could make it Tuesday, at the same time? I've just realized I've double-booked.'

'Right,' Celia said calmly. 'I've got that.'

'If I don't hear from him, I'll assume it's okay. Thank you so much.'

The phone went dead. Celia slowly replaced the handset. She had met Verrall, the presenter of *The Footsteps of Time*, though she doubted he would remember her.

For a moment she forgot all about the apparatus. William had told her about the appointment with Verrall. That was why he had gone out this morning, to see Verrall. That was why he had put on his best suit.

Chapter 19

THESE DAYS TEN thousand pounds wasn't a fortune; nevertheless it was a comfortable sum to have at your immediate disposal. Some of life's luxuries were now within reach. After Dougal returned the keys to the estate agent's, he took a taxi back to Kilburn.

Ten thousand pounds, tax-free and in cash, did have a few problems, though it seemed churlish to worry about them at this juncture. For example, it might be difficult to explain the money to Celia. Nor did he want to arouse the curiosity of the Inland Revenue. The bank-notes themselves would have to be used with caution: presumably Newley's building societies had retained a record of their numbers, which they would have passed to the police.

Various strategies suggested themselves. He could use the notes one by one, for purchases which would be difficult to trace back to him. Or perhaps gambling offered a solution: a lot of ready money changed hands on race courses and in casinos. A third option would be a fake transaction, preferably abroad. He had an old friend in Amsterdam who might be able to help.

Then, of course, he still had the remaining coins, which Lorton had given him. He needed expert advice. There was no point in rushing into anything. The coins, unlike the cash, would not depreciate in value.

He paid off the taxi on Kilburn High Road and walked the rest of the way home. Celia might be curious if she saw him arriving by taxi. The precaution made him feel guilty. He didn't want to deceive her any more than he had already. This would be positively the last time, he promised himself once again; from now on he would be strenuously law-abiding, as befitted a respectable married man.

The resolution, he assured himself, had come into effect some weeks earlier, at the end of his professional association with Lorton. Today's escapade was just a momentary aberration which might legitimately be thought of as the tailpiece to the Lorton business. It was ironic that Celia herself had been responsible for the temptation to deviate briefly from the new régime of moral hygiene. The thought of ten thousand pounds going begging had been too much to bear.

The flat was silent, which surprised him; Celia usually had the radio on when she was alone. He let himself in and walked into the living-room. Her head was just visible, above the back of one of the armchairs. He dropped a kiss on her hair.

'Had a good meeting?' she said.

'Not bad.' Dougal regretted the need to lie. He switched to the truth: 'I'm going to see him again on Monday.'

She stirred in the chair. She was looking at her hands, which lay on her lap. Dougal's cheerfulness dropped away. When you lived with someone, you became abnormally sensitive to changes of mood; communication had flashes of almost telepathic intensity. He could sense that something was wrong.

'It's stopped raining,' he said at last, in a forlorn attempt to paper over whatever crack had opened between them. 'Do you fancy a pub lunch?'

Celia shook her head. 'Gilbert Verrall rang.'

He sat down suddenly in the other chair. An unwelcome crowd of implications rushed into his mind. He knew she wanted him to say something, but there were no words for what she needed to hear.

'He wants to change the Monday to Tuesday,' she continued. 'The same time. Apparently he double-booked.'

Her voice sounded remote from him, as if she was passing a message which meant little to her to a stranger who meant less.

'I can explain,' Dougal said.

'Can you?' For the first time she looked at him. The desperation in her face shocked him. 'Is there someone else?'

'*No!* I swear it's not that.' He left the chair and knelt beside her. He tried to take her hands, but she pulled them away. 'Celia, you must believe me. That's the one thing I wouldn't do.'

'Then why did you lie?' Her mouth puckered. 'And it's not just today, is it? I met Rod this afternoon. He came to say goodbye. He had a message for you: *Tell him it wasn't me.* You two were doing something together, weren't you? And you didn't want me to know.'

'All right, I'll tell you.' Dougal could see the tears gathering in her eyes. 'I've been stupid but I never wanted to hurt you.'

His mind was in turmoil. Part of him hated himself for the wanton destruction of something so fragile, and so important to both of them. Another part was wondering, with shameless objectivity, just how much he need tell her. A partial confession would have many advantages, not all of them selfish. The less Celia knew, the less she would be hurt.

'Will you tell me everything?' she said with sudden savagery. 'Everything? Where you were that day Ivor disappeared? What happened to your coat? What did you steal from Georgina's office? And what about all those intimate little chats with Rod?'

Dougal flinched under the hail of questions. He had the sensation that she was tearing down his barriers with the ruthlessness of a nurse stripping plaster from a suppurating wound; she exposed his soul in all its shivering, messy inadequacy. An overwhelming need to escape flooded through him: he could get to his feet and go, with nothing but his best suit and ten thousand pounds in his pockets. He could be free from all responsibilities. He looked up at Celia's face, and saw the tears spill from her eyes and slither down her cheeks.

'Celia, darling.' He swallowed, yearning for a cigarette, and realized that the decision had been made for him. He no longer wanted to be free. 'You remember the first time I met Rod?' he said. 'It was that dinner party, just before Arabella died. I suppose that's when it started.'

Celia could see the clock on the mantelpiece from where she sat. It had a soft, electronic tick, relentlessly measuring the seconds as they passed. In fifteen minutes, at twenty to three, the two hours would be up.

Why today? she thought. *Why today of all days?*

'Let me get this straight,' she said, interrupting William. 'Rod wanted to get even with Ivor, and you were broke; so you stole some of Ivor's coins, ones he shouldn't have had, and held them to ransom. When you went down to collect the money, you found Ivor's body instead. Why didn't you report it?'

William lit a cigarette. 'Because it would have involved me. The whole business might have come out. And there was another thing: I thought Rod might be trying to set me up. That cheque book under the body might have been his one mistake.'

'*Tell him it wasn't me*? Is that what he meant?'

'I think so.'

'And then you had the idea of framing Georgina?'

'Only after I realized she must have been responsible for Arabella's death. And look what she did to Yorick . . .' He waved the smoke away from her. 'All right. It's not very pretty. But it had a dreadful logic at the time.'

'I see. So you put an innocent woman in jail because it was the logical thing to do.'

At present scorn was the only emotion which buoyed her up. Without scorn she knew she would sink. It was twenty-nine minutes past two.

'That's the strangest thing about it,' William said. 'She wasn't innocent at all. You told me she'd killed Ivor.'

Celia gaped at him. 'How?'

'You said that Fowler-Troon had the Jacobite Guinea, and that he'd got it from Georgina. That was the coin Rod left in the gazebo, as a sort of token of good will. It had vanished by the time I got there. Which meant Georgina must have been there. I think she insisted on coming with Ivor on that Sunday. I doubt if she knew about the stolen coins, though maybe she knew he'd drawn out ten thousand quid. When they got to Miller's End, I imagine he made some sort of excuse and went out. But she followed him. And killed him.'

She stared at him in silence, trying to assimilate what he had said. It suddenly seemed important to disagree with him. He *must* be wrong.

'You . . . you can't be sure about that.'

William shrugged. 'It's beyond reasonable doubt. I reckon she planned it, too. She must have been waiting for an opportunity to kill him. It's the only explanation for the cheque book: she probably picked it up in the office, after Rod resigned. She was trying to frame him for the murder. It wasn't a bad idea: he had a motive, and his background would have gone against him.'

There were nine minutes to go.

'Georgina might have gone there afterwards, and found him dead.' Celia added, not without malice: 'Maybe she didn't want to get involved, either.'

'She didn't want to be charged with murder, it's as simple as that.' William stood up and flicked ash into the ashtray beside the clock. 'The jury convicted her partly because of circumstantial evidence that implied she was there. Okay, that evidence was faked. But the Jacobite Guinea shows she *was* there, after all. If we'd had nothing but the truth at the trial, she'd still have been convicted.' He sucked at his cigarette and stubbed it out. 'That's why I was so happy, the night you told me about the guinea.'

The night you asked me to marry you. Celia banished the memory. 'But why should Georgina kill Ivor?'

'Didn't I tell you? I think he realized that she had something to do with Arabella's death. He tried to phone Georgina, you know, on the night it happened. And she didn't answer. That gave him a substantial reason for divorce. And it gave her a substantial reason for murder.'

Another minute had crawled by. Celia was perversely grateful for the conversation: it prevented her from thinking exclusively about what was happening, or not happening, in the bathroom.

'Perhaps you're right,' she said slowly. 'But it doesn't alter the fact that you stole the coins, blackmailed Ivor and framed Georgina. And what were you doing today? Mugging an old-age pensioner?'

William sat down. 'I suppose I deserve that.'

He looked tired and beaten. For an instant Celia wanted to comfort him, even to apologize for hurting him.

'I went to Steele's Grove,' William said. 'Did you know it was on the market? Rod heard from Maxham that the police hadn't found the ten thousand pounds. The obvious inference was that whoever had taken the Jacobite Guinea had taken the cash as well.'

'Ivor's hiding-place in the study?'

He nodded. 'I thought, if we needed a bigger flat . . .'

'Not now,' Celia said. 'Not ever.'

The clock ticked away the seconds. She counted the ticks, wishing they were sheep to send her asleep.

'I'll burn the money, if you want,' William said. 'Give it to charity, I don't care. Just say the word. But give me another chance. Please.'

She got up. 'I love you, William. But I can't live with what you've done or what you are.'

She went into the bathroom and bolted the door behind her. She would move out this afternoon — go to a hotel or to a friend's. The longer she stayed here, the worse it would be for both of them.

The Perspex box was on the shelf above the basin. The mirror in the bottom of the box reflected the circular base of the test tube. The liquid in the test tube was a pale yellow, tinged with green. The mirror showed it in cross-section. In the middle of the yellow circle was a rust-coloured ring.

Celia was trembling so much that she held on to the wash basin for support. Her reaction took her by surprise. She had expected to feel panic, annoyance or even fear.

Instead she was immensely relieved: everything was out of her hands. Mingled with the relief was a feeling which surprised her even more: a sense of gladness.

William banged on the door. 'Celia. We must talk.'

Talking seemed irrelevant now. Everything was irrelevant in comparison with the simple fact that she was pregnant.